Cherry Blossom Temple

C. L. Shore

Dedicated to my family members, past, present, and future.

CHERRY BLOSSOM TEMPLE

A WORD TO THE READER

This story contains Japanese words and phrases, names of
temples and shrines, and other location names, e.g. cities,
neighborhoods, and streets. When a Japanese word or phrase
appears for the first time, I've italicized it. A glossary in the
back of the volume provides an English translation. The reader
will also find a list of the temples and shrines described in the
novel, which are also italicized the first time they appear. Other
place names, e.g. cities, neighborhoods, and streets are not
italicized.

CHAPTER ONE: JAPAN, DAYS ONE AND TWO

Marissa ran her hand over the sturdy planks before raising the heavy knocker and letting it fall. A deep, hollow sound resounded from the wood.

"Brent," Marissa whispered. "I made it."

A young Japanese woman peeked around the door of the *ryokan*, or guest house. She wore a delicately hued kimono with the traditional wide *obi* belt, but her hair was cut in a modern style. "Welcome back to Kyoto," she said with a subtle bow. "I am called Aoi." She gestured toward her nametag with a movement as graceful as a ballerina's. AOI, with Japanese characters underneath. The pronunciation sounded like "Ahouwee". *Should I add 'san" after it when I speak to her? Like "Aoi-san"?*

"You have a reservation, yes?" Aoi gestured toward a small desk.

"I do." Marissa pulled her rolling suitcase toward the desk. "My name is Shively, Marissa Shively."

"Yes. A room in the north wing has been prepared for you." The young woman bent down and appeared to be looking for something on a shelf. She picked up an envelope with her slim fingers and tucked it in her obi. "You are tired, yes? And hungry?"

"Not very hungry," Marissa said. "I bought a *bento* and ate it on the bus from Tokyo. I *am* tired, though."

"Ah. Your room is ready for you. There's a tea service in your room, of course," her hostess informed her. "And rice crackers if you need a snack later."

"Perfect. I plan to do a little unpacking, but I'll go to sleep soon. I want to be ready for sight-seeing tomorrow."

"Of course. Please follow me." The young woman led her down an adjacent hallway and stopped in front of a wood-paneled door. She pointed to a tile depicting blue and purple blossoms next to the door frame. "Hydrangea room," Aoi explained. She slid open a pocket door and stepped into an anteroom. Marissa recognized the *genkan*, or area to leave her shoes. She slipped off her travel sneakers, and the receptionist stepped out of her platform sandals. Aoi then opened a second sliding door, revealing a simple, uncluttered room. Marissa longed to plop on the plump futon but forced herself to stand as Aoi pointed out the room's features.

"Thank you so much." Marissa bent forward at the waist, surprised at how natural the gesture felt.

"Enjoy your evening. If you need anything, please let me know." The young woman bowed. Her hands went to the sash at her waist. "Ah! I received instruction to give you this." She pulled the envelope from her obi and extended her hand. Marissa's heart thumped in her chest. A letter sent to her at this address? Only a few people knew about her trip, and she couldn't remember giving specific details to any of them.

Marissa bowed for the second time as she took the envelope. Aoi closed both doors quietly as she left. Marissa heard her delicate footsteps as she retreated down the hallway.

Marissa sat gingerly on the side of the futon. The envelope's return address belonged to Lance Jones, Esquire, with a Washington, D. C. zip code. The name sounded familiar. *Brent's lawyer!* She ripped the envelope open, finding a small, yellow sticky note attached to a sheet of thick ivory paper. Marissa tore off the smaller note, scanning the brief message.

Ms. Shively, Brent instructed me to mail this on March fifth of this year, to this Japanese address. Best, Lance Jones.

Marissa smoothed the heavy piece of stationery, unfolding it carefully. *Brent's handwriting*. Her fingers began to shake. She laid the paper on the bed.

Marissa,

You made it! I'm envious when I think of you arriving at "our" honeymoon inn.

I am so blessed to have been your life partner for fifteen years. It was bad luck that our time together was cut short by my illness, but we've had more happiness together than many people experience in a lifetime.

Because you're reading this note, you're fulfilling my desire to return my wedding ring to the temple we visited on our honeymoon. The one we nicknamed the "Cherry Blossom Temple." I forget its proper name, but I know you will find the spot. Please leave my ring there, in the pool under the bridge where the water's surface was covered with cherry blossoms from that giant tree. I hope you can travel when the cherry blossoms are at their peak.

By this time, you will have found the prepaid credit card underneath this note. Use it for a memento. Maybe the Mikimoto pearls we didn't have time to shop for? Or something unique that symbolizes this trip for you. Whatever you choose, it's fine. You've been through so much the last couple years. I appreciate you sticking with me through thick and thin. We almost stretched the "thin" to the breaking point, but your resilience came through and always saved the day. You're my hero.

I love you.

Brent

Marissa peeked in the envelope. Yes, a credit card was inside. Given the expenses surrounding Brent's illness and all the financial crises that followed, she was both surprised and touched that Brent could provide her with any additional funds. She bit her lip. Tears streamed down her cheeks as she shook her head. The ryokan was so quiet, she felt certain even muffled sobbing could penetrate its walls. She returned Brent's note to the envelope. The perfusion of her tears made reading impossible now. She flopped back on the futon and rolled onto her side. After forcing herself to take a few deep breaths, she opened her eyes. The ryokan-provided sleepwear, a one-size-fits-most garment, lay on the futon's surface a few inches in front of her nose. The tiny snowflake pattern reminded her of a hospital gown, something she'd seen Brent wear far too often. She forced herself to take another slow breath, feeling the air expand her lungs. She'd known her journey would be emotional, but she didn't expect her feelings to erupt so dramatically on arrival.

A few seconds of fumbling among her suitcase contents produced the tiny satin box containing Brent's wedding ring. She placed the red case on the dresser and propped

Brent's letter against it. She would reread it tomorrow, and probably every day, for a long time.

***

You're my hero.

The phrase was front and center in Marissa's brain as her eyes adjusted to the faint light. Brent thought *she* was a hero? Incredible! He had been the strong one, even as the weight poured off him, even as he retreated to lounging on the window seat most of the day. She'd been a sniveling mess through much of his illness, angry a lot of the time. Not angry at Brent, but at the cancer that was sucking his life away.

She'd slept on the half of the futon closest to the door, with her suitcase still open on the floor. After digging around in one of its pockets, she retrieved a tiny velvet pouch. It held Brent's wedding gift to her, a necklace featuring a platinum pendant of the infinity symbol. She'd wear it today and every day until she found the cherry blossom temple and its pool where she'd leave Brent's wedding ring.

She filled the electric tea kettle with water and plugged it in. After rifling through the tea offerings in the small basket, she chose one that smelled both floral and subtle. A delicate blossom floated to the surface after Marissa added hot water to her cup. She inhaled the unique fragrance.

Marissa tugged at the tie on her ryokan-issued pajamas. She'd opted to sleep in the neatly folded garment wondering if refusing to wear it might be taken as a partial rejection of the ryokan's hospitality. She felt better about sleeping in it when she realized it was decorated with cherry blossoms, not snowflakes. She sipped her tea and re-read Brent's letter. So like him to be both sentimental and practical. Those qualities were the yin and yang of their relationship. The practical became so dominant, at the end, a side effect of his illness she hadn't anticipated. A tear threatened to roll down her cheek. She brushed it away. *I need to get ready for the day. Can't afford to waste temple-finding time.*

She put on the pendant and went into the adjoining bath to brush her teeth. Tears flooded her eyes when she caught the glint of the infinity symbol in the mirror. Brent had placed the pendant around her neck after toasting her at their rehearsal dinner. She turned up the water volume to cover her sobbing, thankful she'd opted for a room with a private bath. It took several minutes for the deluge of tears to slow to a trickle. Marissa splashed cold water on her face and dressed quickly.

She removed Brent's wedding ring from its box. Its inner surface was engraved with their wedding date and a phrase Brent had chosen. *Full circle*. She'd come back to the site of their honeymoon. She'd come full circle.

A cluster of Japanese businessmen exited the breakfast area as she walked in. Two shot a quick glance in her direction. Marissa shrugged. She was an American and traveling alone, did the combination make her unusual? She saw an empty seat at the counter and took it. *I'll try and sit with someone at a table tomorrow. But today, I'm in a hurry.* A young man wearing a simple white shirt and black pants placed a cup in front of her before pouring green, fragrant tea into it. *Sencha*, Marissa guessed. The flavor of the Japanese tea was exquisite, she'd have to take some home with her, and locate a tea importer once she returned to the Washington D. C. area.

She savored the delicate hot brew. The waiter also set down a bowl of brown, cloudy broth. Marissa tried it, finding the flavor strong and salty. The young man returned with a plate and set it on the counter. A small fish flanked a perfect mound of steamed rice and a concoction resembling a rolled omelet took up the rest of the plate. Marissa wasn't wild about the idea of fish in the morning, but she decided to give it a try. It was fresh and hot, and she enjoyed the rice and egg, with their complementary flavors. The broth was not her favorite, though. The waiter refilled her teacup. She was aware of a few glances from other diners, but her thoughts prevented her from paying much attention. Thankfully, the Japanese were too polite to stare.

On the way back to her room, she picked up an official Kyoto map in the lobby. Although it was mostly in Japanese, it did feature some English. She found the hand-drawn map that Aoi had given her the night before. It displayed local landmarks within a few kilometers of the ryokan and the notations were in English. In addition to featuring the temples, castles and other historic landmarks, it also pointed out restaurants and laundromats. The illustrations were hand-drawn in a clever, edgy style. Someone probably had fun designing it, but a notation in the corner warned "not to scale."

She turned her attention back to the official map on its heavy, laminated paper. She spread it on the table surface in front of her and laid the hand-drawn version next to it. She noted the location of the famous *Kinkaku-ji*, or Golden Temple, on both. She'd start her quest there. Kinkaku-ji was not the cherry blossom temple that she and Brent had especially liked, but it was a place they'd visited on their first full day in Kyoto. She'd do the same today.

Brent's wedding ring would stay in the room for now. Once she'd found the location for its new home, she planned to make a specific trip for her private ceremony of leaving it. Today would not be a good day anyway, no sunshine, and the cherry blossoms were still in tight buds. She imagined the ideal day should be sunny, bright and breezy, with the cherry blossoms raining down on the little pond. Plus, she needed some time to mentally prepare before parting with the ring.

The walk to the Golden Temple appeared to be simple and direct, according to the photocopied map. The exact route was a little hazy in Marissa's memory, but she knew she'd pass a pansy-covered wall before making a turn. If it was still there, of course. Enough local businesses were located on the map that she should be able to validate her path. She put both maps into her tote and pulled out her Japanese phrase book. She quickly reviewed the section concerning questions about locations. She felt confident about her ability to ask, but less sure of her ability to understand the answers.

The massive size of the ryokan's door effectively blocked out street noise. Once outside it, a jumble of pedestrians, bicyclists and motorized scooters competed for space on the narrow street and even narrower sidewalk. A gong from one of the nearby monasteries added a note of calm to the bustle of a workday. The sky was a little hazy, but the bright light above signaled that direct sunshine could appear. Marissa checked her tote for sunscreen and sunglasses before continuing down the path.

The pansy-covered wall appeared after Marissa walked a few blocks. She marveled at the care someone had taken to craft the wall itself, deposit the soil in its multiple stone pockets, and plant the hundreds of flowers. The pansies appeared to be thriving, cascading down the wall in a riot of colors. A star-shaped intersection of three streets was only a few meters beyond the floral display. Marissa remembered how the lack of right angles in this part of Kyoto had disoriented her on her honeymoon. She had always regarded herself as well anchored in the art of finding her way around, but she quickly realized that her abilities were aligned with the predominance of the right angle in street intersections. In some neighborhoods, Kyoto's streets branched off here and there in various directions and met up with other streets at odd angles. She decided that making the turn was what she needed to do. If she was correct, a laundry and a restaurant should be visible in the next block.

She'd been right in turning the corner. After passing the restaurant and laundry, Marissa saw a sign with an arrow, indicating the Golden Temple lie ahead. Her feet started to move faster. *Must be related to my relief at arriving in Kyoto and setting out what I came to accomplish.*

Compact businesses and homes lined the narrow sidewalk. Many had earthenware pots of flowers at the door. The Japanese attention to beauty was something that had struck Brent on their honeymoon visit. "A geranium at every doorstep," he'd said. Marissa could almost hear Brent speaking the phrase. Funny, she'd forgotten that detail. Her return to Kyoto had unlocked a treasured memory.

Several blocks later, Marissa wondered if she'd missed a turn. She hadn't encountered the Golden Temple although other temples were visible along the street. A group of uniformed Japanese school children swarmed across the road at the corner ahead. Maybe they were headed to the same destination. After crossing the street behind the group, she noticed the Museum for World Peace sign. The school group was obviously headed for a different place.

Retracing her steps, she saw the familiar green and red logo of a Seven-Eleven. Brent had joked about the ubiquity of convenience stores in the Japanese urban areas. They'd picked up multiple meals there while traversing Kyoto on their honeymoon. They'd agreed that some of the convenience stores' food offerings were healthy, and they were fresh, too. Of course, you could find the salty snacks and ice cream as well. Brent had become addicted to a Japanese version of the ice cream sandwich: green tea ice cream between two waffle-like layers.

Approaching one of the young male clerks, she delivered her much-practiced question about the Golden Temple's location: "*Kinkaju-ji wa, doko desu ka?*" He responded enthusiastically in Japanese. She cocked her head as she tried to process his response and he began an animated pantomime. She stifled the urge to giggle when he appeared to be performing a shuffling moonwalk in a forward direction. From his gestures, Marissa guessed that she was close to the temple. She should continue in the same direction for about three more blocks. At least she hoped it was blocks and not kilometers. Marissa heard the Japanese word for "three," but the clerk also repeated a word that sounded like "poon" and she didn't recognize it.

Marissa thanked him with "*Arigato gozaimasu*," and left the store, continuing in the same direction. Within a block, she saw signs with arrows pointing ahead, and two blocks later, she saw the entrance to the park surrounding the Golden Temple. Crowds of people, mainly school children in uniforms, babbled with excitement as they streamed through the narrow entry. Immaculately uniformed guards pointed the way to a small lagoon with their white-gloved hands. The still water mirrored the beauty of the iconic golden building on the other side of the pond. "We're really in Japan," Brent had said to her on their first visit. Yes, she was really back in Japan, retracing the steps taken on her honeymoon.

Marissa marveled at the temple's beauty, as she had when seeing it with Brent. Sparse white and pink blossoms flanked the temple, and a few green leaves were budding here and there. After observing the stately building from across the lagoon, she rounded the temple, ending up behind it. The area featured delicately landscaped grounds with statues interspersed with the shrubs. One grouping of sculptures resembled different representations of Buddha. Some were slim and dignified; but a larger, rounded one dominated the garden area closest to the walk. He wore a jolly facial expression and a small pot had been placed in front of his plump belly. Children were throwing coins at it, and a few of them landed in the bowl's depression, making a ringing sound.

Marissa decided to try her luck, ignoring the inner voice that told her throwing coins was a waste of good money. She threw a ten-yen coin at the statue. The coin hit the Buddha's head and bounced behind the figure, out of view. She tried a heftier five-hundred-yen coin, aiming carefully and focusing on her hollow target. She was rewarded by a resounding gong-type sound that echoed a few times. Several adults and children in the immediate area applauded. Her luck was one more sign that her journey was blessed. She was meant to be here on this day.

After touring the remainder of the grounds, she stopped at a concession stand near the exit for some green tea ice cream. The weather continued cool and misty, but ice cream could be the cure for the hunger pangs gnawing at her stomach. A group of school children gathered around her with notebooks in hand as she collected her green cone. She guessed they were about twelve to thirteen years old. All were wearing navy pants or skirts with white shirts, probably their school uniform.

"Excuse me," the tallest boy said. "We would like to ask you some questions. Is it okay?"

"Yes, it is fine." Marissa smiled at the collection of dark, bright eyes surrounding her. "I hope you don't mind that I am eating. My ice cream is melting."

The boy nodded and began asking questions about where she was from. Several of the taller children exchanged glances when she told them she hailed from the United States capital. Pencils wiggled as each of her responses was carefully recorded in their notebooks. At the end of the interview, the children took pictures with her after politely asking permission. The smallest girl asked, "Who is with you?"

The question took Marissa aback for just a moment. She placed her hand on the infinity symbol pendant. "One other person. But he is not around, right here, at this time."

The girl appeared to accept Marissa's vague explanation and took something out of a small satchel at her waist. She offered Marissa a gift of seeds in a colorful envelope, presenting them with a little bow. Marissa felt like a celebrity. Her mood, which had already been optimistic, soared even higher. In spite of her anxiety about making this journey, all was proceeding well.

She watched the children move toward the gate to exit. Her hands were sticky after eating the ice cream; she searched her purse for a wet towelette. Finding one, she unwrapped it and wiped her hands, scanning the area for a trash container. She looked over the courtyard and trees, and inwardly jolted when she met the eyes of a middle-aged Japanese gentleman. His direct gaze struck her as an inquiry. Marissa had the feeling that she'd seen him before but dismissed the thought as an impossibility. *I'm an American in the midst of Asians. I'm sure that I stick out.* Her cheeks burned, she hoped she wasn't blushing. She glanced toward the ground, before sneaking a glimpse back. He was still looking in her direction. She noted he was wearing a business suit and a hat, probably not a teacher with a group of students in tow. The hand furthest from her reached up and touched the brim ever so slightly while his eyes remained focused on hers. Was the gesture a method of communication with her? If so, it was Western, not Asian. She felt flustered for a fraction of a second, not sure if the man was expecting a response. She managed a fleeting smile in his general direction before refocusing on the task at hand, finding a waste container.

Marissa exhaled once she reached the public sidewalk. She sighed, realizing that she'd been breathing shallowly for the last few minutes. Her right index finger traced the outline of the infinity symbol on the chain around her neck. She retrieved the maps from her tote, scanning the names of the other temples in the immediate area. One of them might be the cherry blossom temple of her honeymoon experience. But how to know which one? This day was a little gray, a little cool; not at all like the bright sunshine of their honeymoon. The cherry blossoms still hid in their tight buds, making her search even more confusing. Maybe she should wait a day or two. On the other hand, she could go through a few temples today, to see if any chord of recognition would result.

Retracing her steps, she reached the entrance to the *Ryoan-ji* temple. She looked toward the zen garden from her position on the sidewalk.

After the day had started out on such a bright note, Marissa felt her mood plummet. She had been so sure that her intuition would lead her to the right spot, even though that wasn't her goal for the day's explorations. Her mood, which had been so positive at the Golden Temple, had turned melancholy in an instant. If she failed in her mission, she'd find it difficult to forgive herself. The thought of taking Brent's wedding ring back home made her eyes fill with tears. Ryoan-ji would need to wait for another day.

She retraced her steps toward the guesthouse. Her

energy level had crashed along with her mood. It was well past noon and the sugar high from the green tea ice cream had worn off. She stopped at the same Seven-Eleven where she'd asked for directions and bought two *onigiri*, or rice balls. She'd become addicted to them on her honeymoon, and she *was* hungry.

When she returned to the ryokan, a carafe of tea sat on a table in the entryway. She poured herself a cup, then moved to the small interior courtyard where she sat on a small bench, viewing a tiny pond. She could hear the gentle flow of the brook nearby. "Brent," she whispered. "Please help me. I'm feeling very lost without you now." She watched the orange, black and white koi dart among the lily pads in the courtyard pond, while eating her small meal and drinking the fragrant tea. The peaceful surroundings helped her despair give way to a calm sensation. She went to her room and pulled the shades. Jet lag could be the source of her negativity. She'd nap a little and head to one of the local restaurants for dinner after refreshing herself.

CHAPTER TWO: JAPAN, DAY TWO

Marissa splashed some water on her face and ran a comb through her hair. She applied a hint of blush and lip gloss, appraising her face in the small mirror. Hopefully, the dark circles under her eyes would be gone the next morning. She looked presentable enough to venture out and find the curry restaurant she'd passed the previous night. It struck her as a casual place.

Outside the *ryokan's* heavy door, the narrow gravel path continued to bustle with pedestrians and cyclists. A couple walked in front of her, and she tried to follow the rhythm of their strides, hoping to stay out of the cyclists' path.

"Excuse me."

Marissa turned to find a man with a hat at her elbow. He quickly removed the hat for a moment, before replacing it over his shiny black hair. "My name is Tanaka, Takeshi Tanaka. I saw you at breakfast this morning. We are staying at the same ryokan."

Marissa managed to stifle a gasp. She recognized him as the man at the Golden Temple. His sudden appearance suggested he may be stalking her. She hadn't noticed him at the guesthouse, but the fact he was staying there also made her feel a little more comfortable. "Hello." She said tentatively. "I notice that you speak English very well."

"Thank you." His lips curved upward slightly before his expression became serious. "My family sent me to Harvard for my MBA. I was immersed in English for a couple of years."

"Oh." Marissa struggled to think of something additional to say. "That makes sense." She felt like biting her tongue. *What an inane comment.* And she hadn't introduced herself. "My name is Marissa Shively."

"Pleased to meet you," Takeshi said. "Are you taking some exercise?"

"Well, I guess I am, but I am out to get some dinner as well. I was going to try the curry place not far from the train station."

"Good choice." Takeshi nodded. "Do you mind if I accompany you? I was headed out to get a meal myself."

"I don't mind." Marissa wondered if she should be

alarmed, but she only felt surprise. Was he trying to pick her up? She doubted it. And if he was, she could dissuade him.

He guided Marissa through the small park with its tidy gravel paths and landscaped gardens, eventually arriving at the gate that connected with the city sidewalk. Two blocks later, they were at the door of the curry restaurant, with its wide front window practically on the sidewalk.

Fortunately, the menu had pictures. The curry place reminded her of a Denny's; casual and family friendly. She asked Takeshi about the types of meat in the pictured entrees; as tired as she was, she did not feel like tackling anything too unusual. He indicated that several of the curries were vegetarian. When the waitress arrived, Marissa pointed at one that looked safe enough, a tomato-y looking sauce and vegetables. She also asked for hot tea. The waitress looked puzzled and Takeshi spoke a few words to her in a muted voice. After he gave her his order, the waitress bowed and left.

Marissa felt Takeshi's gaze scrutinizing her in a discreet manner. She wished she had taken more care with her hair and traded her slacks for a skirt. Still, his expression was pleasant, so his opinion couldn't be too negative. Maybe he was portraying an attitude of neutral acceptance when inwardly, he felt repulsed. *You're so good at the negative self-talk. Besides, why does his opinion matter?*

"Have you been in this place before?" She felt more comfortable breaking the silence.

"Not this exact location. But this is…how you say…chain," Takeshi explained. "There is a restaurant like this, not too far from my apartment."

"I see." Marissa paused before continuing. "The waitress looked confused when I ordered hot tea."

"Yes. Typically, curry is served with cold beverages in Japan. But I explained we wanted the hot tea, and they will provide it. I wonder if you have headache?"

"Ah!" Marissa realized she'd been gently rubbing her forehead with her left hand. She dropped it to her lap. "Not a headache exactly, but I do feel a little strange. Jet lag, probably." Marissa didn't want to talk about herself in too much detail. She was relieved to see the waitress approaching with a tray bearing a teapot and two cups without handles. After setting them on the table, the server bowed and retreated.

Takeshi grasped the teapot's handle. "This tea may help you feel better. Allow me." He filled a cup and set it in front of Marissa.

She lifted it and inhaled the delicate fragrance with a deep breath. She felt her shoulders relax as she took a sip. "This tea is delicious. It has a slightly nutty flavor, it's different from anything I've tasted before."

Takeshi's expression was almost a smile. *He looks pleased.* "The tea is called *sobacha*. It is made from roasted buckwheat. No tea leaves involved."

Marissa noted his own cup was empty. "Would you like me to pour some for you?"

Takeshi seemed taken aback by her question, but he nodded and said "Of course."

Marissa felt herself blush. She filled his cup and moved it toward him. Together, they raised their cups and drank.

Takeshi returned his cup to the table. "I was surprised that you chose tea. Most of my American associates want their colas, even with non-American food."

Marissa drained most of the small cup. She'd bought high-quality imported tea in the States since her honeymoon; a special treat she'd enjoyed about once a month. But this tea was far superior in its smoothness and flavor, and it was served in an inexpensive curry house chain! The tension in her forehead was gone. She studied Takeshi as he drank the tea, his eyes briefly hidden from view. He wouldn't stand out in a crowd, but she thought he was good-looking in an understated way. His grooming was impeccable, his clothes were classic and fit him perfectly. His fingers were long and slender, with his nails uniformly manicured. He was slim, as were many of the Japanese, and sported a few gray hairs among the jet-black ones. Marissa guessed he was five to ten years older than she was, but it was possible that he was even older. She'd noted some Japanese people seemed to age very gracefully. Once again, Marissa wished she'd changed into her skirt, which would have hid the little roll of fat that had migrated to her waistline. She hadn't exercised much in the year since Brent's death.

Takeshi broke the silence. "I rarely see Americans traveling alone unless it is for business. But you do not seem to be a businessperson. Are you traveling for pleasure?"

His question took Marissa by surprise. She'd heard the Japanese were very reserved about discussing emotion. She could say "Yes" as the easy answer to Takeshi's question, but that wouldn't be the truth, and would most likely require more explanation. She set her teacup down and looked across the table into Takeshi's face, hoping she didn't appear rude.

"I apologize if I make you uncomfortable. But the truth is, my husband died a year ago. He wanted me to come to Kyoto and return to a certain place here. Now, I hope I can find it."

For the briefest second, Takeshi looked puzzled, or was he offended?

Marissa continued. "It was a place we visited soon after we were married, a temple with a cherry tree in bloom, here in Kyoto. I'm hoping I can recognize the location. I planned the trip so carefully, I'm a little concerned because the cherry blossoms aren't in bloom yet. According to the resources I studied, they should be blooming."

Takeshi nodded, his expression serious. "Predicting when the cherry trees will bloom can be difficult. There are approximations for every year, but the blossoms are capricious. It has been very cool and wet this spring."

Marissa felt her heart sink. She wondered if her face betrayed her dismay.

"But the trees are loaded with buds," Takeshi continued. "They will bloom soon." He consulted his cell phone. "Tomorrow continues cloudy with threat of rain. But next day, bright sun is predicted. I think the trees will bloom that day." His voice sounded confident. Marissa wondered if he was putting on an act for her benefit.

The tension returned to Marissa's forehead, and she started rubbing it in earnest. "I'm on a tight time frame. I will only be here for a week."

"Maybe you can extend your visit, if necessary."

Marissa shook her head. "I can't. One of my friends is

getting married soon. I need to be back for her wedding."

"Ah. I understand. Weddings are important. I am here, in Kyoto for the wedding of my nephew. I'm calling on clients in Kyoto while I'm in the area."

"That is exciting. I can imagine weddings are different here." Marissa tried to banish her worry about the cherry blossom temple to the back of her mind. She'd discuss her concerns with Helen later, via email.

"True. I have been to two American weddings. The Japanese traditional wedding is quite different. My nephew's wedding ceremony will be traditional, but a modern reception will follow. Western-type receptions are becoming more common in Japan, even in Kyoto."

The waitress set their curries in front of them. Marissa was relieved to see a spork-like eating utensil had been provided, and not chopsticks. She could be efficient with chopsticks, but she preferred to wait another day before tackling them.

Takeshi took a few bites of his curry. He balanced his eating utensil delicately across his plate before taking a sip of tea. "How will you find your temple? From what you said, you don't remember its name."

"I think my heart will lead me to the place."

Takeshi's features took on an appearance of shocked

surprise before they rearranged themselves to suggest neutral acceptance. He picked up his spork in his slender fingers. "I don't think I've heard anyone express a plan in quite that way. But perhaps Americans are more likely to trust their hearts."

"You sound skeptical."

"Skeptical may not be the right word. But you must remember, I am a businessman. I look at the world as a businessman."

Marissa realized that she was feeling defensive. "I'm not totally without a plan. I have all the souvenir brochures from my honeymoon with me. And some pictures we took."

"That sounds like it will help."

"Of course, many of my brochures are in Japanese."

Takeshi took a few bites of his curry. "I'm sure the innkeeper would be willing to assist you. She's skilled in English and likes to help guests." He smiled briefly. "Also, she is my cousin."

"Oh! So, that is why you're staying there. I will ask her. Thank you. Now, let's talk about you. What kind of business are you in?" Marissa didn't want to reveal any more about herself than she already had, and this Takeshi was virtually a stranger, after all.

"My family has had an import and export business for a long time, more than a century. But lately we have been expanding into American markets."

"Ah. Hence your American education! Actually, I grew up in New England and went to a women's college there. Some of my high school classmates went to Harvard." Marissa felt like biting her tongue. *Didn't I just say that I wasn't going to reveal more about myself?*

"I enjoyed New England. Parts of the Maine coast reminded me of the fishing villages of Northern Japan."

"Do you ever return to America?"

"Yes, I have clients there. Mostly on the coasts, but in a few other cities, like Chicago, as well."

"Your job keeps you busy, then." Marissa took a few bites of her curry. It was quite good. The food must be freshly prepared, or she was very hungry. Or both.

"Yes. That is one reason why I came to Kyoto early, instead of waiting. I can see several clients, but the occasion will also allow me to enjoy the hospitality of my cousin and relax a little."

"And you said your home is in Tokyo?"

"Yes. I have an apartment there, and my family home is in an old neighborhood on the west side. Fortunately, we weren't as affected by the war as much as some families."

"The war..." Marissa was unprepared for discussion about World War II. In the States, it rarely came up in conversation, unless you were talking with a history buff or veteran. She was ashamed to acknowledge that she didn't know much about the Japanese experience of the war. But, unless Takeshi looked extremely young for his age, he must have been born well after the war was over.

"The war brought Tokyo much damage. We have rebuilt and recovered. Life has gone on." He'd finished his curry and leaned back slightly in his chair. He gazed out the window, watching pedestrians on the street. Marissa decided to avoid commenting about the war and poured him another cup of tea.

Takeshi took a deep breath before speaking again. "My brother is the eldest son, but he really didn't have much interest in the family business and became a physician. It is his eldest son who is getting married. I did have some interest in the import/export business, and as the second son, I will inherit my father's place as head of the company one day. For now, my father is still running things."

"I see." Marissa wasn't sure she really understood, but it seemed an appropriate thing to say. There were still family businesses in the United States, but she suspected that their number must be decreasing every year. She only knew one person in her high school class who had plans to stay with a family business. And then, of course, there was Brent.

Marissa wondered if Takeshi's role allowed him little time to relax, or even to think about having a family. She wouldn't ask him that though, she felt certain such direct questioning would be considered rude.

She finished her curry. "I think I will go back to the ryokan now. A good night's sleep sounds wonderful. Maybe tomorrow I'll feel more in tune with the local time."

"Yes, you'll feel better after sleep." Takeshi stood and put his hand on the back of her chair. "Just to remind you, no tip required in Japanese restaurants."

"Oh! Thanks. That's something I didn't remember."

They were back on the street. The sun still hovered above the horizon, but its light was fading, and clouds were looming to the west. They retraced their steps toward the arch separating the park-like area from the city street. Once within its confines, Marissa noted a monk raking gravel into concentric circles with care.

"Why is he raking now? If it rains, won't his efforts be in vain?"

"Of course. But permanence is not the purpose of the

raking. The person performing the task must be acutely aware of where he is in space and time. He is truly in the moment. That is the purpose. It is a reminder that the present is fleeting. Every time I see this activity, I ask myself about my current place in life. Is it a good place? Is it where I am meant to be?"

"Oh!" Marissa said. She felt like continuing with "what a lovely idea." She couldn't bring herself to say it aloud. Where was she in her life? She was not living in the present, she was living in the past. Could the fulfillment of her mission allow her to take an unfettered place in the here-and-now? Even Brent's letter stressed the importance of getting on with her life.

A wave of sorrow washed over her without warning, giving her no time to defend herself. She struggled to contain her emotions and directed her thoughts to focus on the scene in front of her, a path in Kyoto, a monk raking gravel. This specific spot was where she was meant to be at this point in her life. She wondered if her current location in space and time was the gateway to something of significance, a threshold of some kind.

Takeshi was looking at her with guarded curiosity. She realized she had stopped walking along the gravel path. "I'm so sorry. Many feelings came over me just now."

"Perfectly understandable."

She started to walk forward, and Takeshi matched her,

stride for stride. "You might want to think about doing some alternate sightseeing tomorrow, if the weather is bad, and the cherry blossoms don't cooperate. Uji is interesting, and only a short train ride away."

"I guess I could think about that..." Marissa let her voice trail off. They'd reached the guesthouse. She did have an interest in Uji, a professional one. Uji figured prominently in her dissertation, finished sixteen years ago. But she'd keep that information to herself, for now.

"I hope you have a restful night's sleep. And, by the way, this *ryokan* serves a good American breakfast as well as excellent Japanese cuisine." Takeshi bowed. "Good night." He headed down the hallway to the south wing. She turned to the north side. The hallway was quiet, only the sound of the brook greeted her when she slid open the door to The Hydrangea Room. She found her futon rolled open, with the bedding folded down and the guesthouse sleepwear atop the linens. Marissa had a few tasks to attend to before she could give into the temptation of the plump mattress.

Her unpacked suitcase needed to be addressed, for one thing. Marissa rearranged her clothes into categorical stacks, and put the stacks into a deep dresser drawer, underneath the tea service. She found the folder that contained her honeymoon souvenirs and separated the pictures from the brochures and pamphlets. In the morning, she'd peruse them in more detail and enlist the help of the innkeeper in deciphering the information printed in Japanese. Marissa also resolved to find a detailed map of all temples in Kyoto. If necessary, she'd check them off, one by one.

She'd sleep better if she decided on a plan for the next day before nodding off. She could take Takeshi's suggestion and head to Uji, but she hated to waste time when the side trip didn't pertain to her mission. However, a lack of blooming cherry trees would frustrate her in her search for her specific temple. Getting the perspective of distance might be helpful. And the trip might help her claim a tax deduction, if she used it for academic research. She'd sleep on it.

She caught a glimpse of Brent's blue eyes from the glossy photograph she'd unpacked with her honeymoon souvenirs.

Good night, my love. I'm thinking of you.

CHAPTER THREE: BEFORE

What would have happened if Helen hadn't insisted on going to Joe's Bar?

Marissa had been afraid to jinx her dissertation defense. She had some vague ideas of a sophisticated celebration, maybe a lobster dinner. A few months previously, she'd imagined a romantic candlelit meal with Ron, the history grad student she'd been dating. But once it became clear that Marissa would earn a PhD before he did, Ron disappeared from her life. "Good riddance," Helen had said. "If he can't be happy for you, you don't need him." Marissa didn't make specific plans in case she didn't pass the intimidating defense ordeal. Just as well, Helen wouldn't hear of an upscale dinner. "Get ready – we're going to Joe's! I'm calling Sandy and Jenn."

Marissa looked at herself in the full-length mirror on the closet door. The gray blouse and black skirt she'd worn to face her academic advisors didn't seem appropriate for a bar. "Should I change clothes?"

Helen rolled her eyes. "Yes, you should change clothes! Jeans would be appropriate. Something casual." She giggled. "Nothing that would be hurt if a little beer gets spilled on it."

"Okay." Marissa's jeans were in the bottom dresser drawer. She looked through her meager collection of tees and sweaters. Maybe she'd wear the long-sleeved shirt she'd received after running a ten-kilometer race a few months back. She thought its gold color accentuated the red highlights in her hair. It was also comfortable, and washable. She quickly changed and brushed her hair. "Ready, I think."

"Okay." Helen put her cell phone in her purse. "I just heard from Sandy. She and Jenn will meet us there. Let's walk. It's only six blocks, and that way no one has to be the designated driver."

"Okay." Marissa felt a little hesitant. Was Helen planning on getting smashed? She hoped not. She'd never seen her roommate in an inebriated state, and it probably would only take a few drinks. Marissa decided she'd order everyone some appetizers, too. She was glad she'd gone to an ATM right after her academic meeting; she had a reasonable amount of cash in her small shoulder bag.

Helen held the door open, and Marissa stepped onto the small stairway landing. She'd visited several student friends in modern apartments, but she loved the fact that the place she shared with Helen was once part of the upper story of a large single-family home. She knew the room she and Helen referred to as the sitting room was once someone's bedroom and its fireplace, now decorative only, was once used to keep the occupants from freezing on a winter's night. Her own tiny bedroom was probably once a servant's sleeping quarters. The stairs to the front entry were a little cock-eyed, but that made them even more charming. The little panes of beveled glass in the front door were a detail missing from modern apartments. She sighed. *I'll probably be moving within a few months.*

Marissa perched on a stool at a high top with her three boisterous friends. This was supposed to be *her* celebration, but she felt distant from the banter going on around her. She hadn't considered how finishing her degree would end a phase of her life. The four of them had commiserated and celebrated together for the last three years. Her change in status could bring tremendous changes in those relationships. Oh, things would look and feel almost the same for a while. But changes were set in motion, she could sense their presence. *Stop it*, she ordered herself. *You're sabotaging your own party.*

She ordered herself to stop staring at her half-filled beer glass. Although it was still early, the place was starting to fill up. A couple of gray-haired men in shirtsleeves and ties occupied a table by the front window, their blazers slung behind them. Two younger couples in matching tee shirts sat on stools flanking the bar's right-angle corner. A pair of muscular guys were in earnest conversation a few tables away. It looked like a debate between philosophy majors, but there were only women's colleges within a ten-mile radius. Marissa shrugged and turned her attention back to her friends.

"You guys just come from softball practice?" Marissa asked Jenn and Sandy. They were both wearing their jerseys.

"Yes, finished not too long ago. How about joining the team, now that your dissertation is behind you?"

"Hmmm. Don't know about that. Maybe."

"Speech!" Sandy requested. At first Marissa thought about declining, but she realized her friends were proud of her. She should be proud of herself. She cleared her throat.

"Well, what can I say? You have been the best of friends, encouraging me, listening to me vent. Helping me to have fun while working on this crazy dissertation with its phases and rewrites. I'm grateful, so grateful for your support. I'm also feeling a little sad, because a new phase is beginning. We'll see where that leads." Marissa felt her eyes starting to water. "Yeah, I'm feeling very sentimental right now. But our food is here so let's eat, before I start crying." A server placed a tray of mozzarella sticks and potato skins on the table, along with sides of marinara sauce and sour cream.

"Here, here!" Helen said in a husky stage whisper.

Marissa picked up a mozzarella stick and dipped it in the marinara sauce. The outside was crunchy and hot, the inside was smooth, and the sauce was the perfect tangy accompaniment. Marissa rarely allowed herself fried food, but this was tasty and satisfying. As she glanced down to pick up her beer glass, she noted that her tee shirt was sporting a glob of marinara – right between her breasts. She picked up a napkin and tried to blot up the thick red liquid, thankful the shirt had a logo across the front, at least. Maybe the spot wouldn't be too noticeable. She turned to the right to carry out the clean-up with some degree of discretion.

As she looked up, she caught the eye of one of the muscular men several tables away. He was cute; Marissa noticed his intense blue eyes. *Just my luck. I make a fool of myself and the cutest guy in the place is watching*. He gave her a slight gesture, a subtle raise of both shoulders while lifting his right forearm, palm up. The gesture seemed to say, "Don't worry, things happen."

Marissa looked directly into his eyes. For once, she did not feel tempted to look away from the gaze of a stranger. His gesture, his expression indicated he understood her. His glance went straight to her soul.

"Earth to Marissa." Helen tapped the table in front of her. "Come back. You don't have to decide your entire future tonight." She raised her beer glass. "Let's celebrate."

Marissa forced a smile in Helen's direction. "Okay." She picked up one of the potato skins and bit into it. Good! And there was no dipping sauce to complicate things.

Sandy and Jenn were describing a triple play that had ended one of their softball games earlier that week. Their description became loud and animated and Jenn left her chair at one point to re-enact its conclusion. The activity drew some attention from surrounding patrons. Marissa took advantage of the noisy commotion to sneak another peek at the two men at the table, especially the one with the blue eyes. He was looking over toward their group, but not specifically at her. *Darn.*

Jenn and Sandy continued relating softball anecdotes, and Helen listened intently. "I'm not very athletic, but you two seem to have so much fun. Are there some cute guys on the team?"

"You bet." Jenn laughed. "When you're a student at an all-female college, you've got to find some male companionship somewhere."

Helen caught the eyes of Sandy and Jenn before turning

in her chair to face Marissa. "Well, Marissa you've achieved the holy grail of academia. The doctorate. In recognition of that lofty achievement, we've each selected a little gift to commemorate the occasion."

Jenn cleared her throat. "I want to thank you for being my running partner. We had great conversations during our runs, and you've helped me with my studies, too. You've been my mentor." She brought a small gift bag to the table surface. Marissa looked inside and drew out the contents: A silver bracelet with a charm, miniature running shoes.

"Thank you. What a beautiful surprise, Jenn, you're so considerate."

Sandy was next. "I know how much you've sacrificed for your academic career." She placed a colorful envelope on the table. Marissa opened it. It contained a gift certificate for a local spa. "You deserve some pampering, Marissa. You've worked very hard."

Marissa felt tears sting her eyes.

"Don't cry, don't cry!" Helen laughed. "This is going to bring a smile to your face, for sure." She produced a small rectangular package, the size of a paperback.

"Okay..." Marissa tore off the wrapper. Yes, it was a book. The title was *The Handbook to Fetishes.* "What the heck?"

Helen was really laughing now. "Well…you said your dissertation contained references to these things. You said *The Tale of Genji* could be subtitled *Little Book of Paraphilias*."

Marissa joined in the laughter. "You're right. I could've used this book a lot earlier!"

They polished off the beer and appetizers. "Any more?' Marissa was relieved when her companions indicated they'd had enough. A server appeared and started to clear the table. Marissa stood and retrieved her purse from the back of her chair. She gasped when she realized the blue-eyed stranger was at her right elbow.

"Sorry, I didn't mean to startle you." His voice was soft, and clear.

Marissa noted the glance between Helen and the others, the slight tilt of Helen's head toward the door. The trio moved away from the table.

"Are you an athlete?" He asked.

Marissa laughed and shook her head. "Well, my two buddies are on a softball team." She indicated the running logo on her shirt. "And I try to run twenty miles a week. But mostly, I'm a student. Or was a student."

The stranger gave her a quizzical look.

"I just defended my dissertation today."

"No kidding! I did that just over a year ago."

"Really! What's your field?"

"Informatics. And yours?"

Whoa. Marissa always felt overwhelmed by the math and science types. "Mine's Comparative Lit. "

The stranger put a hand on the back of Marissa's chair. "Listen, I don't want to hold you up. And I almost never do this." He handed her a scrap of paper with the name Brent Shively and a phone number hand-printed on it. Marissa did not recognize the area code.

"It's okay." Marissa explained her need to make sure Helen got home safely, because they'd walked the six blocks to Joe's together. "Let me check with my friends. I might be able to sit and talk for a while."

She ran outside to the neon-lit sidewalk. Jenn and Sandy offered to give Helen a ride.

"I think he's safe," Marissa assured them. "He just finished his graduate degree a year ago."

"Hmph." Helen sniffed. "Sociopaths are very good at persuading others that they're just like them."

"I can trust him. I know it."

"Do you have your cell phone?" Helen wanted to know.

"Yes."

"Let me see it."

Marissa sighed audibly and retrieved her phone from her purse. "Okay, Mom! Here it is! I'm staying. I'm a doctor now, and the doctor is telling you to go home and get some sleep."

Helen shrugged her shoulders. "Okay, guys, let's go. Seems like a Prince Charming has arrived." She gave Marissa a quick sideways hug and a wink. "Be home by midnight."

Marissa watched the trio get into Jenn's car, before she turned and re-entered the bar. She felt very relaxed, and it wasn't just the beer. Brent was sitting on Helen's vacated chair, facing hers. His companion had moved to the bar, where he watched the television behind the bartender's shoulder.

Marissa walked toward Brent, noticing how broad his shoulders were. She reclaimed her vacated seat and turned to face him. "Are you from this area?"

Brent grinned and tilted his head. "Well, yes, and no. I grew up not too far from here. But I live in the D. C. area now. I took the train up to attend a cousin's graduation. Sam over there," he gestured toward the bar "is an old friend of mine from high school."

"Does he have his PhD, too?"

Brent laughed at the question. "Almost."

"The way you two were discussing something earlier, it looked like a debate between scholars."

"Really! Sam will get a kick out of that."

Marissa looked over at Sam, who was nursing a beer and continuing to stare at the TV screen. "He must be a good friend."

"He is." Brent leaned forward. "Now, tell me about you."

"Well, I grew up in New England, too. I'm an only child. I love books, foreign language films and take-out Chinese."

The server brought Marissa an iced tea at her request, but she never touched it. Brent told her he had a successful career in the business world but he found it to be unfulfilling. He got a degree in mathematics and taught high school in an underprivileged neighborhood in Baltimore for a while. Then he went back for an advanced degree in informatics. He was helping his former prof with research while applying for positions. He hoped to land a full-time faculty job at the collegiate level but did not know what his chances were. He told Marissa about how he used to tease his younger brother and trick his next-door neighbor every April Fool's day.

Brent was describing the elaborate prank of his senior year in high school when a server interrupted. "Last call." Sam continued to face the TV screen. The game was in extra innings.

"Sam really is a good friend," Marissa said.

"Yeah." Brent stood. "Can I walk you home? I take it you live close by."

Marissa nodded. "It's only a few blocks."

Brent walked over to Sam and they exchanged a few words. Sam nodded, never taking his eyes off the screen.

Marissa stood up. Helen's gift book fell out of her purse as she pushed back her chair.

"I've got it." Brent stooped to pick up *The Handbook to Fetishes*.

"Let me explain." Marissa gasped. "My friend just gave this to me. It's kind of a joke, related to my dissertation."

Brent handed her the book, wearing a bemused smile. "No worries. I get it. Like I was just telling you, I'm a prankster at heart."

The pink and orange neon on the sidewalk faded as they walked up the hill. "Convenient," Brent said. "You live close to Joe's, so you don't need to worry about drinking and driving."

Marissa laughed. "We almost never go there. At least, not Helen and me. Jenn and Sandy may go after their softball games."

"And you chose Joe's as a place to celebrate?"

"Actually, I didn't. But Helen was bent on going there, for some reason."

"I'm glad."

"Me too. I'm even glad about the marinara sauce."

Brent threw his head back and laughed. "I would have noticed you. Sauce or no sauce."

"This is where I live." They'd reached the sidewalk in front of the old Victorian house that had been subdivided into apartments. Marissa noted a dim light in her upstairs sitting room.

"Wow. This house is a little run down, but it has tons of character."

"Exactly. Sometimes I like to imagine all the stories this building could tell." Marissa put her hands in her jacket pockets and shrugged her shoulders slightly.

"Hmmm." Brent reached into her right pocket and retrieved her hand, holding it in both of his. "Maybe it's time to start a new chapter." His lips brushed the back of her hand, then her cheek. "I want to see you again, Marissa." He looked into her eyes and released her hand. "Goodnight."

Marissa had no memory of walking up the sidewalk or going up the stairs to the apartment she shared with Helen. She did remember trying to sleep with the touch of Brent's lips on her cheek and hand still palpable. The sensation hadn't faded when she woke up the next morning.

CHAPTER FOUR: JAPAN, DAY THREE

The suggestion of light brightened the window shade. Marissa searched for her phone on the blanket: 5:10 local time. *Ugh! The sun rises so much earlier in Japan.* She rolled over and tried to return to sleep, but she knew she wouldn't have success. Well, at least she had about seven hours of uninterrupted shuteye. *Not bad.*

She'd email Helen. Thankfully, the guesthouse had Wi-Fi. The innkeeper told her even the nearby monasteries had internet connections. She grabbed her computer off the countertop and sat on the edge of the futon, waiting for the sign-in screen to appear.

She missed having a girlfriend to call or text spontaneously throughout the day. She and Helen had been friends since their freshman year of college. Their relationship had changed, but not faded, when Marissa and Brent married almost sixteen years ago. Now, Helen was in the final stages of planning her first wedding at age forty. She'd said it was worth the wait: Chad, her fiancé, was the perfect life companion for her. Marissa would attend their ceremony within days of her return from Japan.

She and Helen had a frank discussion about Marissa's place, or lack of it, in the wedding party. Marissa felt apprehensive about her emotions as the wedding would take place exactly 53 weeks after Brent's death. She didn't feel ready to march down the aisle of a church sanctuary as a bridal attendant, and she had a feeling she could count on some antiquated etiquette authority to back her up. However, Marissa made it clear that she planned to attend both the wedding ceremony and the reception. Helen asked Sandy to be her matron of honor, but Sandy was relieved to hear that Marissa would be willing to toast the newlywed couple. Marissa felt she could do a good job with that task, and Helen seemed satisfied with the arrangement.

Marissa struggled with the issue of what to wear. Technically, she'd be past the one-year anniversary of Brent's death, so even the older New England matrons couldn't object to something colorful. She did want her gown to be both tasteful and modest, though. She'd stumbled upon a simple but sophisticated lavender dress, and had it tailored. Marissa had to admit the result was flattering. It hung in her closet at home, awaiting her return.

Hey there, Helen,

I miss having you to talk to. Maybe we can Skype sometime soon, if we can work out the time difference.

I'm more than a little disappointed that the cherry trees are not in bloom yet. The weather here is cool and rainy, so the blooming has been delayed. On the positive side, the guesthouse is as warm and accommodating as it was on our honeymoon. It does bring back bittersweet memories, but I'm glad that I decided to stay here. Today, I may go through my honeymoon souvenirs methodically and see if I can find something to help me identify the cherry blossom temple that Brent and I visited years ago.

Last night, I had dinner with a Japanese businessman (and also, most definitely, a gentleman). Turns out, his relative runs this guesthouse. Anyhow, it was interesting, being the dinner companion of a member of the male sex. Felt kind of strange, but partly due to the cultural differences.

How are the wedding plans coming? Since you're into the final count-down, I hope all the arrangements are coming together well. Have you had your final fitting for the dress yet? You'll look amazing, I have no doubt.

Take care. Make sure you get your beauty sleep! Marissa.

After sending her email, Marissa noted that the window shade was darker instead of lighter. Was it going to rain? A loud clap of thunder confirmed her suspicion. She flopped back onto her pillow. Maybe she could catch a little more sleep. No urgent need to scramble around for an early morning sight-seeing expedition.

She rolled over on her side, wishing the shade on the window would brighten. She remembered the dream she'd had just before awakening, a dream of Brent and the night they'd met. His posture, his openness had made Marissa want to run to him and feel the soft fabric of his tee shirt against her cheek. She could imagine the scent of clean cotton, the sensation of smooth cloth against her skin. Brent had impressed her as both open and protective, and her first impression had been dead-on. His goodnight kiss, really just a soft brush of his lips on her hand and cheek, struck her as the most romantic kiss she'd ever experienced.

Another loud clap of thunder, with lightning this time. Marissa stirred, realizing that she'd been close to dreaming. Returning to a restful sleep would be impossible. *Might as well get up and head to the dining room for breakfast.* She'd try the American breakfast this morning but resolved to give the Japanese version at least one more try during her stay.

She found her wrinkle-proof travel skirt and a short-sleeved blouse. She had a pair of shoes that were reasonably waterproof, a jacket with a hood and an umbrella. However, she didn't plan to spend a lot of time outdoors, at least, until it stopped raining. She grabbed Brent's folder of souvenirs and pictures. Maybe if she had a chance, she'd talk with Takeshi's cousin and get her impressions of the photos. The ryokan owner might be able to help her identify the temple she was seeking.

A half dozen people occupied the small dining area. A trio sat at one table, the other diners appeared to be traveling alone. Marissa resisted the temptation to sit at the counter. She approached a table where a middle-aged Japanese woman sat. "May I join you?" Marissa gestured toward a chair at the table. She hoped that the woman understood English, or at least, her gesture.

"*Hai,*" the woman said. She bowed and gestured toward the chair with an open palm. Marissa gathered that the woman was agreeable to sharing the table. "*Watashi wa Marissa Shively,*" she said. She'd been practicing the formal phrase of self-introduction, now she had the occasion to use it.

"Ah," the woman answered. "*Watashi wa Sachiko Nakamura.*"

"*Hajimemashite.*" Marissa felt a little panicky. She'd exhausted her Japanese vocabulary.

A server brought a tray of fish, rice, a bowl of slightly

cloudy broth, and the rolled omelet to their table, setting them in front of the Japanese woman. Mrs. Nakamura paused and put her hands together as if in prayer. The server looked at Marissa. "American?" he said.

Marissa nodded. She wasn't sure if the server was asking if she was American, or if she wanted the American breakfast. The server left the table, and Mrs. Nakamura said a few brief syllables and gave a little bow toward her plate. Her food looked more like a dinner than a breakfast, Marissa thought. The Japanese woman picked up her bowl and sampled the broth.

"What is that called?" Marissa asked. "I tried it yesterday. It was a little salty for me."

"It is *miso shiru*, and many Japanese meals start with it, including breakfast." Mrs. Nakamura said. "For foreigners, it may be an acquired taste."

The server returned with two cups on a tray, one tea, and one coffee. The coffee was set in front of Marissa. Probably because coffee is part of the American breakfast, she thought. She tasted the brew and found it to be excellent, dark and flavorful without noticeable acidity. She wondered if it was freshly ground. The server came back with a plate of scrambled eggs, link sausage, and one perfectly round pancake. He set the plate in front of Marissa, then gave a subtle bow before leaving. Marissa imitated Mrs. Nakamura's little bow toward her plate and picked up her fork.

"I welcome the chance to practice my English," the Japanese woman said.

Marissa quickly swallowed the bite of egg she'd tasted. "Thank you. I don't know much Japanese, so that helps. You speak English very well."

"What brings you to Kyoto?" Mrs. Nakamura asked.

Marissa didn't want to go into her entire story. "Well, I am here to return to a place I've been to once before, in the cherry blossom season. I want to see it again."

"I see." Mrs. Nakamura sipped her tea. "A happy place?"

Marissa nodded. "Yes, most assuredly, a happy place."

"I hope you find it, then. Did you find the place alone, the first time?"

"No." Marissa tried to find a way out of the question. "But the other person couldn't make the trip. I'm making this journey for both of us."

The answer seemed to satisfy Mrs. Nakamura. She nodded her head and sipped more tea.

Marissa judged her companion to be about fifty years old. She was dressed attractively and wore a delicate strand of pearls that appeared to be of high quality, maybe Mikimoto. The words *sophisticated* and *refined* fit her perfectly, Marissa thought.

"I've been enjoying the local Japanese tea. But this coffee is good," Marissa announced. "In fact, it's excellent."

Her breakfast companion smiled. "Takeshi Tanaka sees to that. His company imports this coffee and sells it to the ryokan at cost. He's related to the owner." Mrs. Nakamura smiled as if sharing a private joke with someone unseen. "He could stay at the most expensive hotel in Kyoto, yet he chooses to stay here."

Whoa. So, Takeshi Tanaka is a rich man. Makes sense, his clothes are so well tailored and they're probably also very expensive. Marissa felt her cheeks burn, hoping they weren't flushed to the point that Mrs. Nakamura would notice. She wondered if he really frequented that curry restaurant chain, he probably made the comment just to make her feel more comfortable. *Why go to Denny's when you can afford Ruth's Chris every night?* She fought the urge to shake her head.

"Oh, you know Mr. Tanaka?" Marissa couldn't resist the chance to collect a little information about him.

"Oh yes, I've known him for many years. I happen to work for a rival import/export company. Our paths cross from time to time, sometimes at this very place."

She smiled. "But ours is a good-natured rivalry. Plenty of business to go around." She changed the subject. "You are traveling alone?"

Marissa sighed without thinking about it. She hoped her breakfast companion would not regard her as rude. "Yes, I am traveling alone. I am a widow. I came to fulfill a request made by my late husband."

"I am sorry. I don't mean to intrude." The Japanese woman put down her chopsticks and regarded Marissa with concern before lowering her eyes.

"Oh, please don't worry. I don't mind telling you." Marissa said. "It has been almost a year since he died."

The Japanese woman nodded. "I also am a widow. My husband departed almost ten years ago. I miss him still. But life goes on, and I am happy to have my daughter and my grandchildren to visit."

"Are you in Kyoto to visit them?"

"Yes, for the most part. But I am also enjoying some time to myself. Japanese dwellings are very small, making it difficult to entertain guests in the home. So, I am glad to come back to this guesthouse in the evening. I have some books to read. And I will spend one day shopping."

"Does Kyoto have good shopping?"

"Oh, my!" The woman covered her mouth with her napkin. Marissa guessed Mrs. Nakamura was hiding a smile. "Kyoto is well known for its fashionable shops. There is a Japanese saying: You can go broke in Osaka buying food, but you will go broke in Kyoto by spending too much on clothes."

"Ah." Marissa tucked that piece of information away. Maybe if she found the temple in good time, she'd shop for some clothes. She'd bought nothing new, except for the dress for Helen's wedding, since Brent had died. It was probably time to update her wardrobe.

Mrs. Nakamura had finished her breakfast. She performed another bob of the head toward her plate with hands pressed together. "Marissa-san," she said after rising from her chair. "It was good to meet you."

Marissa experienced a second of panic. As the older person, Mrs. Nakamura should be addressed with a title of respect. *Should I call her Nakamura-sama?* Unsure of the proper term of address, Marissa used the formal *thank you* phrase, "*Arigato gozaimasu*. It was good to meet you as well. Enjoy your day."

"Thank you. I think it is going to be a wet one."

Marissa finished her breakfast and drained the last of the excellent coffee. Rain continued to pound on the roof, and the darkness outside the windows suggested it was the middle of the night, not the beginning of a business day. It would be a wet one, indeed.

Marissa left the dining area and searched for the innkeeper. Finding her in the foyer, she asked her if there were any references available about the temples in the Kyoto area. "I have a few brochures and pictures with me. I think the place I'm looking for has a bridge with red railings."

"Many temples have bridges and red is a common color in temples," Takeshi's cousin said. "But I have something that may help you." She walked behind the desk near the entryway and looked at the volumes on a bookcase. She found a large book and pulled it off the shelf. "An American gentleman brought this book with him a few years ago. When he left, he gave it to me, saying he would not be back to Kyoto again. He thought another American might find it useful." She smiled and placed the book on the counter. "I think that other American is you." She placed the large book with its colorful jacket on the desk. "Keep it as long as you need it."

Marissa picked up the heavy volume. "Thank you. I will return it to you." She resisted the urge to sprint back to her room and walked sedately instead. Once inside, she sat on the futon and began to rifle through the pages.

The book contained exquisite photographs, most of them in color. Temples were depicted in various times of the year. Cherry blossoms were featured in some photos, but autumn leaves and snow were visible in others. She also found a map, with the various temples noted by stars in all parts of the city. She tried not to panic when she saw the number of them. Surely, there would be a way to prioritize the likely locations. She needed to keep her head together. This book could be a valuable resource in helping her find the Cherry Blossom Temple.

The sky was still dark. No thunder had sounded for a while, but the pounding of incessant rain on the roof continued. Takeshi was probably correct when he said that the cherry blossoms would not bloom today. Maybe it would be a good idea to get some perspective on her task, as he'd suggested. She'd go to Uji and take the book with her. After touring the temple there, she'd find a place to enjoy some tea and study the pictures. She'd develop a plan. Marissa's sensation of helplessness shifted to purposeful action.

Her waterproof backpack was folded tightly in the outside pocket of her suitcase. She put the book in a plastic bag first, as an extra precaution against the rain, before placing it at the bottom of her backpack's largest compartment. She added her compact umbrella and put on her raincoat. Time to head to the train station and find her way to Uji.

CHAPTER FIVE: JAPAN, DAY THREE

The subway came above ground and followed a wide river flanked by rocky banks. Rough-hewn boulders gradually became smaller until they comprised the gravel of the river bottom. Ten minutes later, the train pulled into the Keihan Rail station at Uji. Mountains framed the opposite side of the tracks. Takeshi had been right, Uji was only a short jaunt from Kyoto. Marissa followed the crowd toward the town center and the bank of the wide river. Rapids danced in the shadow of the long bridge spanning its breadth. Thankfully, the rain had moderated from a deluge to a trickle. Marissa kept the hood up on her jacket but left her umbrella in her bag.

Marissa turned to her right, as the innkeeper had directed her. The statue of Murasaki Shikibu, author of the world's first novel, *The Tale of Genji*, sat serenely with the swift-moving waters behind her. She didn't seem to mind that she was soaking wet. *Genji* had been written over a thousand years ago; Marissa had been impressed that a woman had written this early work. She'd tried to read the English translation as a college sophomore but got lost in the myriad of characters and the lack of an apparent plot. She'd been intrigued enough, though, to compare analyses of the work for her doctoral dissertation.

Brent had found Shikibu's novel on her bookshelf a few months prior to their wedding. Evidently, he'd heard that *The Tale of Genji* had a reputation for being a racy tale. Brent had jokingly said it would be good preparation for a Japanese honeymoon. However, after struggling through a few chapters, he acknowledged that a lot of the eroticism must have been lost in translation. "Maybe I should read Helen's book of fetishes instead." Marissa laughed aloud at the memory of dropping the paperback at Joe's Bar. A few bystanders turned her direction and she quickly covered her mouth.

To her Western eyes, the statue of Shikibu looked very sedate, even nun-like. She appeared to be wearing several veils, or maybe the long, sculpted folds symbolized her hair. Marissa had read that the multiple layers of clothing indicated wealth. Shikibu held a scroll in front of her, as if reading. Her features expressed serenity. *So much for appearances*.

Marissa followed the signs toward the Uji's *Byodoin* temple, passing a line of shops and small restaurants.

Most of them had closed doors and rolled-up awnings. A shopkeeper in the closest establishment dragged a meter-tall plastic ice cream cone to the sidewalk. Another shopkeeper hovered near the window. He eyed Marissa with an expression that conveyed suspicion as she walked past. She wondered if he'd witnessed her spontaneous outburst of laughter earlier. If so, he may think she was a crazy woman. The mental image of herself erupting into giggles made her want to laugh even more, but she managed to control the impulse. She glanced at the shop windows as she walked toward the temple, looking for potential small souvenirs to take home. She also appraised the cafés, perhaps she could enjoy some tea after touring the temple. Several were positioned between the shops, and activity within them signaled they would likely be open before too long.

The lane of shops and teahouses ended at the boundary of the temple grounds. A dozen schoolgirls, wearing navy blue pleated skirts and white sailor blouses, clustered around the entrance. Marissa enjoyed their excited chatter even though she couldn't understand the content of their speech. Their enthusiasm about the day's excursion was obvious and infectious. An adult man and woman accompanied them; they appeared to be paying the fees for the group. Marissa found her yen in her backpack and paid the entrance fee. Signs in Japanese and English warned against photography and even prohibited sketching.

Marissa dawdled behind the schoolgirls. She followed them through the outdoor courtyard to a platform where a large bell hung under a protective roof. Evidently the sign in front of the bell gave permission to ring it using a suspended piece of lumber that reminded Marissa of a battering ram. A couple of the schoolgirls tried. Ringing the bell appeared to require effort, but they did meet with success. Several giggled nervously at the bell's deep, solemn sound while others remained silent. One young girl wore an awestruck expression, her eyes wide.

 Marissa approached the area near the bell when the school group moved on. She decided to pass on the bell ringing and looked across the small pavilion to the reflecting pond and the row of shops she'd passed earlier. A few minutes after the school group had passed through the temple doors, Marissa entered. *I must concentrate. The images I encounter must stick with me. Like the monk with his rake, I must be in the moment.* She was greeted by an altar area, featuring a statue she assumed to depict the Buddha. The ornate altar contained fruit and flower offerings arranged in artful clusters. After passing through the area dedicated to worship, she encountered a gallery displaying banners featuring calligraphy and delicate paintings. Finally, she entered an area selling souvenirs. She paged through a book with detailed photographs. Since she couldn't take her own pictures, the purchase of the book seemed a good investment.

The sky was still gray and the air moisture-laden when Marissa exited the museum. At least the rain had stopped. She followed the lane back to the row of shops and tea houses. Savory fragrances announced that some of the establishments sold food. She returned to one of the cafes she'd noticed and entered the display area where tea was sold in bulk. Marissa's stomach rumbled in response to the aroma coming from the kitchen. Approaching the counter at the rear of the store, she ordered two hot buns containing a beef filling, steamed rice, and sencha tea by pointing to the picture menu. She waited for her food at one of the few tables flanked by benches. The kimono-clad shopkeeper soon approached with a tray, gesturing to indicate the buns could be hot.

 Marissa nibbled on some rice, after poking holes in both buns with her chopsticks. Her server was right, steam escaped from the vents and she could feel the heat on her wrists. After sipping some of the tea, Marissa cautiously bit into the first bun. The filling was slightly spicy and still very warm, but safe to eat without burning her mouth. Her gnawing hunger satisfied for the moment, she settled herself with the pot of tea, the book about temples, and her pocket-sized notebook.

Marissa closed her eyes and tried to retrieve her

memories of that important day with Brent. She remembered the shirt he wore, a madras plaid with short sleeves. She'd worn a casual, flowery dress – chosen because it packed well. Brent happened to like it too, an added bonus. He'd always said he liked the way the skirt showed off her legs. They'd visited several temples that day, their special one might have been the third they'd walked through. It definitely wasn't the first one they'd encountered. She remembered walking through the temple and standing under a larger-than-usual cherry tree that rained blossoms on the two of them, and onto the surface of a small body of water – a pond, most likely. They'd stood on a bridge, under the canopy of the huge tree and snapped a photo of themselves by extending Brent's hand holding the camera, a selfie with his Nikon.

"Marissa-san?" A male voice came from close by. "Are you feeling all right?"

Marissa looked up to see Takeshi standing before her. She felt her eyes open a little wider and her jaw drop slightly before she regained her composure. "Takeshi! I mean, Tanaka-san. I'm well, thank you. Just a little tired."

Takeshi exchanged a few words with the owner, who brought a large pot of tea and a second cup. The owner poured a vivid green brew for him from the new pot. Takeshi inhaled the steam rising from the small cup before taking a sip. "My company supplies the tea for this establishment. You've made a wise choice in coming here if you like the finest. Uji is known for its tea, as well as for its temple."

Marissa felt her shoulders relax a little. "Ah. Explains the lane of tea houses, I guess. This particular brew is excellent." She gestured toward her cup.

"Yes, I noticed you were drinking *sencha*. I chose the *matcha*, it is grown locally. Uji is famous for its matcha."

Takeshi was wearing a black suit with a white shirt and charcoal tie. His clothes gave him an air of sophistication, and the suit looked exceptionally well on his lanky frame. Marissa felt rumpled in her raincoat and casual attire. *My hair must look a fright, after the rain and humidity.*

Takeshi pointed at the volume in front of her. "I see you have a book with you."

Marissa closed the book and held it so Takeshi could see its cover. "Yes, your cousin provided it. It's written in English, and maps out many temples in Kyoto, with at least one picture of each. I'm doing some research."

Marissa detected a subtle upturn in the corners of Takeshi's mouth. Then he gestured toward her cup with his palm. "You have the lucky leaf."

"Excuse me?" *The lucky leaf?* Marissa couldn't imagine what Takeshi was talking about. Maybe she didn't hear him correctly. "Would you mind saying that again?"

"The lucky leaf. In your tea."

Marissa gazed into her cup. A few leaves floated on the surface. One was sticking up. She touched it with her chopstick. "Is this what you mean?"

"Yes, to have a tea leaf pointing above the surface of the liquid, that is considered very lucky. I would take it as a sign that your strategy is a good one."

"Really!" Marissa did feel her mood lift. *Strange, I'm letting my mood be influenced by a single, nonconformist tea leaf.*

Takeshi drained his teacup. "I must be going. I have clients to call on."

"Thank you for suggesting Uji. I've enjoyed this side trip. I just hope I can remember some of the amazing artwork I saw today. I was surprised about the ban on photographs, and even sketching. I've never seen a sign like that before!"

"Yes, that is a strict rule about parts of the temple's interior."

"You mean I could have taken pictures of the outside?"

"Yes. But do not worry, you may have picture of the temple in your pocket now." Takeshi's smile was subtle, but it lasted more than a few seconds.

Marissa wondered if Takeshi was talking in riddles. "I don't understand."

"Let me explain." Takeshi produced a leather pouch from his pocket. He found a coppery-looking coin, roughly the size of a quarter, and held it out in his palm. "The ten-yen coin pictures the Uji temple. Always keep one and you can look at *Byodoin* whenever you want."

Takeshi bowed slightly before turning toward the door. Marissa felt her heart beat a little faster. He was so elegant. And polite. Especially polite.

After taking a few steps toward the entrance, he turned back to Marissa. "The sky is looking lighter toward the west." He bowed again and left as two patrons entered.

Marissa poured herself more tea and opened the temple reference book to its inside cover. A jumble of numbered dots appeared superimposed on a map of Kyoto. Most dots were red, about a quarter of them were green. The legend said the red ones represented temples and the green ones indicated shrines. *Over eighty temples!* She'd have to scrutinize their descriptions and pinpoint the most likely ones. Marissa doubted she could visit them all in the small amount of time she had.

Marissa quickly rifled through the pages of the book, hoping for a jolt of instant recognition on some of the pages. There were a few temples with red and green details, and she recorded their page numbers in the small notebook she'd brought with her. She looked carefully at the temple views depicted in springtime. She couldn't say any one of those was the special one, although she was able to rule out several. She made a note of those in her book as well. Her confidence increased a little. She was developing a plan, making some progress. She'd compare her notes with Brent's jottings in the folder back in the room at the *ryokan*. After looking for additional views of the temples online, she could select those most resembling the temple in her memory and make a list, then circle their locations on the map. In pencil, of course.

Marissa drained her teacup and returned the book and notebook to her backpack. She looked in her purse for money, before remembering she'd paid for her meal when it was ordered, and there was no tip to deal with. She nodded to the owner, who smiled graciously. Although she had been served with utmost deference, the server's attitude had changed dramatically when Takeshi had appeared. *I guess Takeshi has a reputation around here, a good one. Maybe he's something of a local celebrity.*

The sky had brightened in the last hour. Marissa ambled along the line of storefronts, moving toward the bridge and the train station. She stopped in one shop and purchased two pairs of ornate chopsticks for Helen and her husband-to-be. Before leaving the area leading to the temple, Marissa lingered in front of Shikibu's statue. The author of the early novel looked even more serene and elegant in the brighter light. Marissa looked behind Shikibu's image, toward the mountains screening the true horizon. She could see the beginnings of a rainbow forming between their peaks.

Tomorrow could be a sunny day.

CHAPTER SIX: JAPAN, DAY THREE, EVENING

The afternoon train teemed with passengers. People poured into the cars at each stop between Uji and the Kyoto main station, resulting in jostling and crowding. Marissa didn't mind standing, but the curious stares made her feel a little uneasy. Two children peeked out from behind their mother but hid behind her skirt when Marissa smiled at them. Thankfully, the ride back was as short as it was crowded.

 Marissa stopped at the Seven-Eleven adjacent to the Kyoto station and picked up a shrimp and rice noodle salad for dinner. She felt exhausted by the scrutiny she received as a solitary Caucasian traveler throughout the day. She craved the chance to lounge in privacy, plan her next day's activities, and enjoy a Skype conversation with Helen. After kicking her shoes off in the genkan, she flopped on the futon. Resolving to make tea in a few minutes, she tried to conjure up an image of herself with Brent on that day in the Cherry Blossom Temple, more than fifteen years ago. She closed her eyes to improve her concentration but found herself dozing off. *Jet lag.*

She forced herself to stand up. She felt drowsy, but she needed to eat her dinner and stay awake to acclimate to the current time zone. She plugged in the teapot and looked for a packet of green tea; something to improve her concentration, but not interfere with sleep later. She'd skim through her email and maybe even outline an article about Shibiku and the *Tale of Genji*. Then she'd study her temple book and use the internet to research the locations that looked promising.

An image of Brent sprang into her consciousness. He was wearing the red tee shirt he'd worn at Joe's. She remembered how that shirt smelled like it had just been taken down from the clothesline on a sunny day. He'd had this rough-and–tumble appearance, like an endearing small boy who'd just come in from a game of tag football.

Takeshi's polished sophistication was quite a contrast to Brent's casual gregariousness. Then there was Takeshi's calm, serene expression, only occasionally hinting at emotion. Marissa remembered the suggestion of a smile that he'd revealed early that afternoon before quickly rearranging his features. Brent, on the other hand, wore his emotions for all to see. He'd joked that he could never be a poker player. The two men had similarities, though. Both were the sons of wealthy businessmen, and both were involved in the family business.

Stop it! You're comparing Brent and Takeshi, like they're the two major men in your life.

Mrs. Nakamura seemed to be a kindred spirit from another culture. However, she had a child and Marissa didn't. It was funny, Brent had been open to the idea of having children, but when there were none, neither of them fretted about their childlessness. Marissa had seen a couple of her friends become frantic in their quest for a baby. Although she would have welcomed a child, both Brent and she were busy pursuing their careers and enjoying their relationship. They did not feel a void in their life together.

Marissa turned on her computer and connected to the internet. She didn't want any problems when it was time to talk with Helen via Skype. After scanning her university email to make sure there were no student emergencies, she lounged on the edge of the futon. She placed the temple book in front of her and took bites of her salad while leafing through the pages. Setting the empty food container aside, she returned to the map near the beginning of the large volume.

She knew that she and Brent had visited *Nijo* Castle, one of the best-known landmarks in Kyoto, and the scene for much of the action in *The Tale of Genji*. She remembered specific castle details, the moats and the so-called nightingale floors that were constructed to squeak as a defense against intruders. The interior had struck her as very bare and plain, save for the few ornate paintings on some of the walls. She also remembered she and Brent had typically seen a minimum of three or four major attractions in a day, and sometimes crisscrossed the city, instead of staying in one area. Using the castle as the central point for her plan, she looked for temples in the surrounding city blocks. There were several marked on the map. She noted the numbers assigned to them on a piece of paper and consulted the legend at the foot of the page for the name of each one.

Using the index, she looked through the temple illustrations and descriptions. She started a separate column on her paper for this information. She left another column blank. She'd use that space for facts about each temple provided by searching the internet. Finally, she scanned Brent's notes, and the hand-drawn map provided at the ryokan when she'd checked in.

One memory that she'd resurrected, and she hoped had returned to her accurately, was that of the small body of water under the bridge she'd stood on with Brent. It was almost completely hidden by the thick coat of cherry blossoms on that day, so it was impossible to see its outline. The cherry tree on the bank was larger than most they'd seen, the two of them could stand under it without ducking. If she could find that tree and that bridge, she'd know the pond was the intended place for Brent's ring.

The first temple was *Shinzenko-ji*. There was only a small picture of it in the book, and it appeared to have been taken in late fall or early winter. The trees were almost bare; a few dried leaves clung to the branches. However, there was a greenish building in the background. Maybe it also had red trim, it was difficult to tell due to the small size of the picture. She'd add it to her list, the photo held some promise.

The second temple on her list, *Hirano* Shrine, was depicted in springtime with many pale pink blossoms on a single, large tree. Marissa felt hopeful. She couldn't see a red-and-green building though, or a gently arched bridge. Still, she'd make it a point to visit the location.

The third one, *Jobon Rendai-ji*, was depicted in black and white. Trees in the background were in bloom, and there did appear to be a pond in a section of the landscaped garden. Judging from the map, this temple wasn't too far from the second one on her list. Of course, she'd try to visit it, too.

The alarm on her phone jolted her attention away from temple pictures. Time to log on to Skype. She fluffed up her hair and sat tailor style in front of the computer screen. It would be so good to talk with her friend, someone who understood her without a lot of explanation. She was missing a familiar voice to confide in. Her computer indicated that Helen was waiting for her. She clicked on the link.

Marissa fought the urge to do a double take. She recognized Helen's face but her hair had been swept into an elegant, asymmetrical "up do", and her makeup had been expertly applied. Marissa was struck by the lavender tones in her eye shadow and the complimenting blush and lipstick. Helen appeared ready for a TV appearance on a morning news show, or soap opera. Marissa looked at the time and did a mental calculation. It was only 8:30 AM on the US east coast.

"Helen, you look great!"

Helen's smile became even wider." Do you like the 'do? I went to my hair stylist at 7AM, imagine that! I had to bribe him with a giant Starbucks' in hand, plus a gift card. And the makeup person was there, too. This is my look for the wedding. What do you think?"

"I think Chad will be bowled over with your beauty, that's what I think. Are you getting excited?"

"Actually, I think I'm in denial. I can't believe that the wedding is only a week away."

The words brought a nauseating quiver to Marissa's stomach. The wedding was so close, and she had to be there. The fact that her temple search hadn't really started yet was even more distressing considering she must leave Japan on time.

"How's the wedding toast coming?" Helen seemed to be reading her thoughts.

"It's coming along very well." Marissa's cheeks flamed with her bluff, but she rationalized that it was only a little white lie. After all, she'd conducted mental rehearsals of speech content for weeks. She just hadn't written anything down.

"Are you getting enough sleep? You look kind of washed out."

"Well, I'm jet lagged. The time zone shift is huge. But I feel like I'm sleeping fine. This guesthouse is very comfortable." Marissa's embarrassment gave way to annoyance. *Helen knows I hate being told I look tired.*

"How are you doing with your mission? Did you find the temple?"

"Well..." Marissa stifled the impulse to wince. "The fact is...I haven't gotten off to a great start. The weather has been cool and rainy, and the cherry blossoms are not in full bloom. But tomorrow is supposed to be sunny, so I'm hopeful. I have my resources and maps out right now. I'm optimistic that tomorrow could be the day."

"I'm sure you'll find it." Helen's voice sounded superficial. "At least, you've been there before."

"True." Marissa didn't want to focus on the temples. "When's your bachelorette party?" She was glad to have an excuse to miss it. The ritual didn't seem to fit her current frame of mind.

"Two nights from now. I think it will be a kind of sedate affair. After all, most of the attendees are married."

"Don't make assumptions." Marissa continued to wrestle with her irritation over Helen's "washed out" comment. Otherwise, she would have laughed.

"So, other than looking for temples in the rain, what have you been doing?" Helen appeared to be looking at something out of the camera's view.

"Let's see. I've met a few interesting people. The innkeeper, for one, has been very helpful. She even lent me an illustrated book to help me in my search. Yesterday, I met a Japanese widow, who's about ten years older than me. She's very nice and staying at the ryokan, too, for a while. Then I had dinner last night with that Japanese businessman."

Helen's eyebrows raised. "Yeah! Watch out for those Japanese businessmen. Some of them have very antiquated ideas about women. To say nothing about being kinky. Remember that MIT student we met in that bar near Cambridge?"

Marissa sat back. "I don't think Takeshi is antiquated. Or a misogynist, if that is what you're thinking."

"Takeshi! So you're on a first name basis?"

"Well, I think of him by his first name. I don't know if I've called him by that name, though."

"Well, don't! The Japanese reserve first names for close friends only. He may read way too much into the situation if you use his first name."

"Helen, you haven't even met him." Marissa struggled to keep her voice low and calm. She was amazed about the direction the conversation had taken. Helen was succeeding in making her feel increasingly defensive. How could she steer her to a more neutral topic?

"True. I'm just saying Japan is different, and Japanese men are different."

"Well, tomorrow I'm off to the temples and I probably won't see him again." Another little white lie. Marissa realized she had no definite plans to see Takeshi in the future, but she assumed she would, at some point. "What's your day like today?"

Helen gaze drifted downward, toward something in her hand. "Oh no, I've gotta go. Listen, in two days, I'm off work for a couple of weeks. Let's Skype again then, okay? Bye."

Helen's image disappeared.

Marissa sighed and felt her shoulders slump.   She'd been anticipating this conversation with excitement and to say she felt let down was an understatement. She collapsed on the futon and felt tears running down her cheek before she heard herself sob.

She missed Brent.

CHAPTER SEVEN: JAPAN, DAY FOUR

A bright white square outlined the Hydrangea Room's window shade. *The sun must be shining*! Marissa's mood soared before it took a nosedive, as memories of her conversation with Helen flooded her consciousness. She struggled to her knees to view herself in the mirror across the room. *Ugh!* As she'd feared, her eyes were swollen and red. She grabbed two teabags from the in-room tea service, dampened them with tepid water, and applied them to her closed eyelids. She reclined on the futon and mentally reviewed her plan for the day while waiting for the anti-inflammatory action of the tea to take effect. She'd skip breakfast in the dining room and grab something from a convenience store instead. She did not feel up to an encounter with Mrs. Nakamura, Takeshi, or anyone else. After getting ready for her day, she'd slip out of the *ryokan* and head for Nijo Castle. She'd arrive well before temple opening time, grab some sort of breakfast in the area and get her thoughts together. The nearest train station had a line that would take her close to Nijo Castle and she'd find the temples from there. She didn't plan to visit the castle itself, unless she was sure she had located the right temple. Then she might return to the castle to celebrate.

Her eyelids looked better after the teabags had worked their magic. She washed her face to get rid of the tea stains and dressed hastily. After gathering her backpack with the book, her purse, and her sunglasses, she exited her room, double-checking for her room key before reminding herself there wasn't one. She approached the front door of the guesthouse just as Mrs. Nakamura reached the entry to the dining area. Marissa put her sunglasses on and gave her a hurried wave.

The sidewalk bustled with bicycle and pedestrian traffic. The walkers and cyclists seemed a little more relaxed on a Sunday morning, though. The sun had cleared the treetops, revealing a bright cloudless sky. Marissa was glad for her light jacket, but she felt sure that she'd be shedding it in an hour or two. Tracing the familiar route to the closest train station, she consulted the map and bought a ticket. Just as she put it in the turnstile, the attendant bellowed *"Ohayo gozaimasu,"* his voice echoing off the ceramic-tiled walls. Marissa jumped at his voice, afraid she'd done something wrong. She felt dangerously close to tears. A quick mental review of his words reassured her. He'd merely been wishing her a good morning. *Calm down, Marissa.*

Plenty of seats were available on the Sunday morning

train. She exited at the stop for Nijo Castle and climbed the stairs to ground level. Her cell phone read 7:30 AM. She decided to cross the street and walk around the outside of the impressive complex with its protective white wall. Hard to believe the structure was a thousand years old. The age of many of Kyoto's buildings emphasized the relative youth of the United States as a nation. School children, young couples, and businessmen passed her. The modern and the ancient appeared to comfortably exist in the same city block. She'd laughed the previous afternoon when she realized Kyoto's Manga Museum occupied a space in the midst of temples and castles that were built centuries ago.

Marissa did not see any temples from the outside of the castle. She couldn't see any street signs indicating temples were nearby. She made a note of the street adjacent to the Nijo: Horikawa-dori.

Retrieving the official Kyoto map from her purse, and perusing her three columned notes for information, Marissa noted two temples that appeared to be a few blocks north of Nijo. A third area, the Kyoto *Gyoen* Garden was also described as a cherry-blossom viewing spot and was only a few blocks away. The temple farthest from the castle, *Myokaku-ji*, opened at nine. She'd find a place to have breakfast and study her maps.

She saw a doughnut shop on the corner about a block

away. Not the most nutritious breakfast, but it would offer a taste of home.

The place was doing a brisk business. *The Japanese must love doughnuts.* Slim Japanese men in black suits comprised about half of the customers, even on a Sunday morning. Casually dressed young people chatted at tables, the businessmen munched while scanning cell phones. Marissa chose a pink doughnut with blossom-shaped sprinkles on its frosting, hoping her choice would bring her good luck. She found a seat at a tiny table, giving herself an unobstructed view of the street. She'd eat, study her book, watch the people go by, and plan her day.

Her thoughts circled back to her conversation with Helen the previous night. The passage of time should have softened the impact of Helen's words, but Marissa found them harsh and almost accusatory. She had to admit she'd held high expectations, thinking that talking with Helen would help her feel more optimistic and less isolated. Instead, she'd felt miserable and even more alone. Was she at fault, for holding such high hopes? Or was Helen turning into a bridezilla? Or was she, Marissa, just too sensitive due to fatigue, or grief? It was Helen's turn to be in the spotlight.

I should be happy for my best friend. So why do I feel so sad?

CHAPTER EIGHT: BEFORE

Marissa felt as if she'd stepped into a fairy tale while planning her wedding. Thanks to Brent's success in the business world, he'd augmented her parents' modest wedding budget. Marissa found a dressmaker who understood her description of a simple, but elegant, silk dress with a train. The dressmaker's stunning creation surpassed Marissa's imagination and Helen confirmed she looked regal wearing it. Then, Brent indulged her with the smashing sapphire evening gown to wear at the reception. They'd passed it in a store window after completing their wedding registry. Marissa stopped on the sidewalk to remark about the striking blue satin fabric and the off-the-shoulder design.

Brent said, "I'll buy it for you."

What! I'm a college instructor! I don't have a place to wear something like that dress."

"Yes, you do," Brent affirmed. "Our wedding reception."

"But I have the beautiful white gown. I love it. And people will be expecting to see a bride."

Brent grinned from ear to ear. "I'm a believer in the unexpected. You can wear the beautiful white dress to the afternoon wedding and this sexy number to the evening reception. We're holding it in a ballroom, no less – you're entitled to look glamorous in an evening dress." He tugged at her elbow. "Come on, there's only a half hour until store closing."

The size eight fit like it had been custom made for her. The sapphire fabric showed off the red tints in her auburn hair. "Sold!" Brent's declared when she emerged from the dressing room. "You'll be a knockout at the reception. I want every guy in the place to be insanely jealous of me."

Helen's jaw dropped when Marissa modeled the gown for her a few days later, but she staunchly defended Marissa's right to wear it. "The old ladies' eyebrows will go up. And some of the guys might have their own ah…physical reaction. But, hey, it's your day, so flaunt your good looks. Most importantly, the groom approves."

A collage of images comprised Marissa's memories of her wedding day, some soft and fuzzy with others in razor-sharp focus. Helen, as maid of honor, played a key role prior to and during the ceremony. Marissa appreciated her friend's ability to organize the bridesmaids, coordinate communication with the groom's party and assist with the flowers. Helen's serene efficiency went a long way toward calming Marissa's nerves prior to her walk down the aisle.

Most of Marissa's wedding day worries concerned her parents. She was their only child, born when both were in their mid-forties. During her graduate school years, her mother suffered a stroke and her father had been diagnosed with Parkinson's disease. Her mother still had a pronounced left-sided weakness and her father's symptoms included tremors and problems with posture. The ushers saw to it that her mother was escorted to her place of honor in the front pew.

The clearest picture in Marissa's mental wedding collage was that of her father. She remembered approaching the narthex as the organist played the prelude. Hot tears stung her eyes when she saw her dad. He stood tall and dignified in his formal wear. "Marissa," he said, "You look radiant." He extended his arm, proud and steady. "Shall we?"

"No tears allowed," Helen said in a gruff voice as she took her place in front of them. Helen's timing had been perfect. Her command helped Marissa giggle and relax a little. Her father maintained a dignified pace as they processed down the aisle to the wedding march.

When they approached the altar, her mother rotated and turned to face them from her place of honor. She looked twenty years younger, her face luminous. In all the frenzy of wedding preparation, Marissa hadn't considered how joyful and proud her parents were. Their faces told the story.

Brent stood at the altar, with his infectious, ear-to-ear grin. Her memories of the ceremony itself were fuzzy. Time seemed to morph to warp speed. Marissa was aware Brent's brother sang a solo and her cousin did a reading. She assumed she said her vows without a hiccup, because no one said anything about it after the ceremony. As the recessional music started, Brent's *full circle* ring was on her finger. She and Brent were husband and wife.

Her parents and Brent's father followed the wedding party to the narthex where they formed a receiving line. Cupcakes and lemonade awaited guests on the lawn while the wedding party had photos taken. This interlude was the unofficial reception, mainly for the benefit of her parents who found late-night events difficult to attend. The evening reception was still several hours away, giving the bridal party a chance to relax among the guests after the photography session.

Marissa treasured the candid shots taken on the church lawn. In one, her mother hoisted a punch cup of lemonade. Her smile was broad, there was only the faintest hint of the left-sided droop she'd acquired from the stroke. That photo was Marissa's favorite.

CHAPTER NINE: JAPAN, DAY FOUR

Marissa stared at the doughnut crumbs on her napkin, trying to shake the sorrow that gathered behind her eyes. The same Helen who'd told her she looked tired last night had paid her a compliment on her striking appearance almost sixteen years ago. Well, Helen looked gorgeous yesterday. It was her turn to be in the spotlight.

She reflected on her little white lie to Helen about the wedding toast. Marissa acknowledged that she hoped, almost expected, to see Takeshi again. If she didn't have a chance to interact with him before she left Japan, she would be disappointed. Marissa tried to identify the cause of the disappointment. She had to admit, Takeshi made her feel special, in a subtle way. His attention made her feel like she had value. He'd even told Marissa that she made him curious. Maybe he found her intriguing. Helen's disparaging remark brought out Marissa's desire to defend him.

Could Takeshi be viewing her as a victim of some sort, as Helen had hinted? Obviously, as a wealthy person, he would have no motive to rob her. Was he looking for a sexual conquest? Marissa snorted a laugh at the thought. She surely didn't look like a temptress. But her widowed status could make her seem vulnerable. Of course, he could genuinely be interested in her. Possibly, because she was an American woman with connections to New England, the same area of the country where he'd spent time as a student. Why was that so hard to believe?

No doubts about Mrs. Nakamura, though, she was a treasure. Marissa hoped they'd have at least one more conversation in the next few days. She'd try to make it a point to have breakfast in the dining room tomorrow. If her temple searching was fruitful today, she'd ask Mrs. Nakamura about the best places in Kyoto to find clothes. It was about time she devoted some effort to her appearance after a year of avoiding her own reflection every time she passed a mirror.

She fingered the infinity symbol pendant at her neck. Brent had been so generous throughout their relationship, and his provision of unexpected funds for this trip was so typical of his giving spirit. They'd been on a progressively tighter budget the last few years of this life, even before he'd been diagnosed with cancer. When Brent's illness was full-blown, and when he couldn't work, their budget took an even harder hit. Marissa shrugged. Maybe he'd found some cash he'd squirreled away and used it for the gift card. She still wasn't sure how much money he'd invested in it, but the total was probably between one hundred and five hundred dollars. She'd need to find out before she could decide what to do with the funds.

Marissa wadded up her napkin and focused on the open page of the English language temple guide at the center of the reference book loaned by Takeshi's cousin. She contrasted the two-page spread with the map she'd consulted earlier. It featured only a few of the many streets between Nijo and Myokaku-ji. As a result, she'd underestimated the distance to the temples north of the ancient castle. They were more than a kilometer away. If she'd realized her error earlier, she would have had plenty of time to walk and reach the first temple by opening time. She could probably figure out how to get to them by public transportation with an instruction or two. She pulled up the translation app on her phone and typed in a question about locating the nearest bus stop for the line running north and south. She approached a businessman who was standing, preparing to leave.

"*Sumimasen*," Marissa said. She pointed to the translated phrase on her phone screen. She hoped the phrase truly asked directions to a bus stop on the north/south line.

The man gave a little bow and pointed to a red line and a dot noted on her map. He gestured at the shop window to the north. "Bus stop. Two blocks," he said.

Marissa imitated his subtle head nod. "Arigato gozaimasu."

Marissa found the bus stop just where the businessman had indicated. By studying the map in the station and comparing it with her book, it looked like she should get off in three stops. She could visit a temple near that stop and then work her way back toward Nijo Castle, visiting the other sites along the way.

She'd forgotten to ask about the bus fare. She dug in her purse for coins of various denominations in order to be prepared. She followed two young people and watched them drop coins in a box. She found her matching coins and dropped them in. The bus driver didn't look her way, so the fare must be correct, she thought. Either that, or the Japanese used an honor system. No one really scrutinizes the amount. She made her way to a seat that allowed her to view the street ahead. Ten minutes later, she saw a sign for the Myokaku-ji temple entrance across the street and exited at the next stop.

She passed through a gate featuring a greenish roof. Was the temple within the courtyard a red-and-green building? The walls of the structure did contain hints of a scarlet hue. Marissa wondered if the walls would appear more red later in the afternoon, with direct sunlight. Like the gate, the temple featured a greenish tile roof. Marisa's heart leaped when she saw a larger-than-average cherry tree in the courtyard. However, there was no body of water underneath it, and no bridge. *Myokaku-ji* was not the Cherry Blossom Temple.

Marissa walked the few blocks to *Suika Tenmangu* Shrine. Two weeping cherry trees were starting to pop bright pink blossoms within the small courtyard. The shrine itself was tiny, but charming. However, it was too small to be the place Marissa was looking for. Still, she sat on one of the dainty stools provided by the shrine and watched a few of the bright pink blossoms fall. She was the only visitor and the shrine was a place to catch her breath.

The solitude provided a chance to reflect on her recent conversation with Helen. Their interaction was so unlike any they had ever had in the history of their friendship. Marissa had been looking at the scheduled meeting as a chance to reconnect with her friend, instead, she felt as if a rift had been created. Her expectations weren't met, in fact, Marissa felt as if they were destroyed. She needed to find her sunglasses; tears were starting to form. She located them in her tote and let the tears flow behind the dark lenses.

Expressing some emotion helped Marissa relax a little. She realized she'd been methodical in her temple searches this morning and part of that strategy may have been a way to dodge her uncomfortable feelings.

Still, she'd succeeded in covering some ground. Confronting her frustration and allowing herself to cry had helped her feel more focused. Yes, her interaction with Helen had been frustrating, but Helen was under a lot of pressure and facing her big day. Maybe she, Marissa, needed to give her a little grace. Marissa blew her nose, removed the sunglasses, and consulted her map.

Although not found in her temple book, the map indicated the *Shokoku-ji* Temple was close by. She was on its grounds within three minutes. There were no decorative cherry trees within Marissa's view, though. *One more temple to cross off my list.* She began her stroll south, back toward Nijo Castle.

A sign for a convenience store flanked the sidewalk ahead. She bought two *onigiri* and a bottle of milk tea, counting out the correct change without much problem. The variety of Japanese teas available in cans and bottles amazed her, as it had on her honeymoon. She placed the unopened bottle in her bag while she munched on one of the rice balls.

A nagging fear emerged from the back of her mind. Would she fail to recognize the correct temple if she saw it? *Memory can be a fickle thing.* If she came to the end of her time in Kyoto without finding *the* Cherry Blossom Temple, she could return to the site that most resembled the one in her memory, the one that seemed most fitting. She might start a list tonight and rank the top possibility at the end of every day. Returning home with Brent's ring still in her possession would feel like a defeat. But she still had time. *I need to have faith.*

She disposed of the *onigiri* wrapper and drank the milk tea as she continued walking south toward *Nijo* castle. *As long as I'm here I may as well take advantage of the opportunity to see the castle again. I can use the tour as a validation of my memory. But I need to do the tour quickly.* Years ago, she and Brent had encountered an American exchange student from the University of Arizona who wanted to give them an informal tour of sorts, as a kind of practice for a future event. Brent had agreed, and the young man had done a good job. Marissa remembered the arrangement of the castle rooms, leading to the most protected location that housed the *shogun*, when he was in town, and the squeaking nightingale floors. She knew the grounds contained a garden, but Marissa remembered it as rocky and was sure that it was not the place where they'd taken the picture. But she'd look to see if any red-and-green structures were visible from within the castle walls, just to be sure.

Marissa passed through the gate and went to an entry area where she paid the admission fee and rented an English self-guided tour tape for 500 yen. She passed through an anteroom where she exchanged her shoes for one-size-fits-all foam slippers provided by most indoor tourist attractions in the area. A group of four men, three Asians and one who appeared to be American, were also engaged in exchanging their footwear. The American flashed Marissa a quick smile and said either "Hey" or "Hi" before shuffling on to the next room. Marissa took a few tentative steps in her own temporary footwear. A good two inches of empty space flip-flopped behind her heels as she strolled along the polished wood. *I'll need to watch my footing. In the U. S., these mandatory slippers would be construed as a lawsuit waiting to happen.*

She pushed the play button on the tape player and the invisible tour guide told her where to proceed. Once she was in the first viewing area, she could see the group of four men advancing ahead of her. They all listened to tapes as well, and they must have them synchronized. Marissa could see them direct their gaze in the same direction, at the same time.

As the tour proceeded, she found herself passing several chambers, looking rather plain by Western standards. A few tapestries and paintings hung on some castle walls, but she saw a lot of empty space, too. The wood floors did creak, as she remembered. The only detail that struck her as new and different concerned hidden areas for bodyguards to observe for any threats. Marissa felt certain that their informal guide didn't mention those features fifteen years ago.

The castle offered an interesting contrast to the temples. She returned to the tour starting point, and prepared to turn her tape and headset in. The group of four men were just ahead of her. The Asian men spoke in English to each other as they returned their tapes and moved toward the bin on the opposite wall to hunt for their shoes. Marissa did the same.

"I'm glad I brought my red sneakers on this trip. Cuts down on the search time." The American-looking man addressed his comment to her. He had curly reddish-blond hair, a short beard and wore khakis with a navy polo shirt. He gestured with the bright red-and-white high-tops he'd just retrieved from one of the twenty bins against the wall.

"That's a good idea." Marissa stopped searching for her shoes and turned to face him. "Very practical."

"What did you think? About the castle?" The man slipped his feet into the sneakers before kneeling to tie them.

"Hmm. The castle's impressive, and for me, it's hard to believe that it is so old. I've been here once before. I had never used the self-guided tour and learned a few new things today. But mainly, I learned that my memory of this place was pretty accurate."

"Yes. This place is unique. Hard to believe one could forget it." He stood and nodded at Marissa. A western-style nod. "Enjoy your afternoon."

"Thanks. You do the same." Marissa watched him walk out with his three companions before continuing the search for her shoes. The storage bins were numbered but she'd forgotten to take note of the digits above the bin where she'd left her gray flats. After a few minutes of rummaging through containers, she found them under several pairs of men's dress shoes. She'd take a quick look around the garden before heading out into the street.

The castle garden was markedly different from the spot captured in her honeymoon photo. Large boulders surrounded the pond. Marissa noted a single cherry tree surrounded by plants and foliage, but it was too short to stand under. About a quarter of its blossoms were open, though. Marissa took a brisk spin around the garden's gravel path before passing out of the gate and onto the sidewalk. She could see the doughnut shop a block ahead. She hoped that the counter people would have changed shifts. Regardless, she'd stop there for a minute, have a quick cup of coffee before returning to the nearby train station and taking the JR San'in Line west to reach two more temples. She wouldn't have time to saunter through them, but she'd have enough time to scrutinize their features. She needed to make use of the entire afternoon.

So many temples, so little time.

CHAPTER TEN: JAPAN, DAY FIVE

Multiple masculine voices rumbled from the back wall of the breakfast area. A few tables farthest from the door had been pushed together to accommodate the group of a dozen males.

Mrs. Nakamura beckoned from a table for two tucked in the corner near the entrance. "Marissa-san. You are welcome to sit here."

Marissa took the seat across from her. "What is happening? It looks and sounds like something special is going on."

"Very special. The Tanaka wedding is today. Those are members of the Tanaka family." She subtly cocked her head toward the back of the room.

Suddenly, a slim male figure strode past their table and headed for the wedding party. *Takeshi.* He did not stop to acknowledge the two of them. Of course, Marissa had her back to the door. She wondered if it would have been considered rude for him to

deviate any attention from the male gathering at the back of the room. Most of the men seated there were young adults. They were joined by another who appeared to be about Takeshi's age, plus one older man. Marissa leaned forward. "I'm assuming that Tanaka's brother and father are at the table. Which of the younger men is the groom?"

"You are correct about the older men, but as for the groom, I am not sure. It has been about ten years since I've seen him."

"I see." Marissa sat back in her chair as a waiter brought a pot of tea to the table. "American?" he asked Marissa.

"No, not today." The server poured tea for each of them. Marissa took a sip of the pale brew.

Mrs. Nakamura picked up her cup. "You could go to the wedding, if you wish to, Marissa-san. Only the family is allowed in the shrine, but anyone can observe the procession through the courtyard. I hear the wedding will be in Gion. At Yasaka Shrine."

Having a ringside seat to the pre-wedding ceremony sounded appealing. "Really! I had no idea I could do that. Watching the wedding procession would be interesting."

Mrs. Nakamura nodded. "Yes. Traditional Japanese weddings are beautiful, although somewhat solemn."

Marissa smiled. "Marriage is a serious business. Good to have respect for that." She noted the conversation at the back of the room was animated, with a few smiles and the occasional laugh. Probably some good-natured jabs at the groom, attempts to dissipate the nervousness he must be feeling.

A Japanese breakfast was placed in front of her. Marissa was getting used to the fish and egg combination first thing in the morning. "Today is a weekday. In the U. S., most weddings are planned for the weekend."

Mrs. Nakamura set her teacup down. "Yes. Western style weddings are frequently on the weekend in Japan as well. But traditional Japanese weddings could be on any day. There are days that are more favorable for weddings at shrines, these are sometimes called 'Buddha present days'. There are also days known as 'Buddha absent' days, those would not be chosen for a wedding. Today is a Buddha Present day, in cherry blossom season. It is a highly favorable day for a wedding. The family made arrangements long ago to have a wedding today, I have no doubt."

"Interesting." Marissa finished her rice. "I think it's refreshing to think the work week doesn't dominate everything here. And evidently, even the Buddha is entitled to days off."

Mrs. Nakamura smiled. "Yes. I guess one could say that."

"What will you do today?" Marissa asked after placing her chopsticks across her plate.

"I'm going with my daughter and her children to the Kyoto Kimono Museum. Then, we will go to their home. We will read for a while, together. Both children are old enough to read, of course, but they love to be read to."

Marissa smiled. "Sounds like you're making wonderful memories with them."

A scraping noise came from the back of the room as one of the younger men pushed his chair back and stood. He led the rest of the group as they cheered three times using a two-syllable chant.

Mrs. Nakamura leaned forward. "They're congratulating the groom."

"Ah. Everyone seems excited, and happy." Marissa set her cup down. "I was planning on starting my day in Gion, and I'll definitely do that now. I saw Yasaka on my map last night. Isn't it one of the more famous shrines?"

"Yes, Yasaka is the most famous shrine in the Gion

district. I don't know the exact time of the wedding, but I think it will start sometime between 10 and noon, based on conversation I overheard. There are other temples and shrines in the area. Many things to see in Gion."

"Sounds like a good plan. I'll leave soon for Gion and start walking around the area surrounding the shrine. I've marked several Gion area temples on my map, so I'll be killing two birds with one stone."

Mrs. Nakamura looked puzzled.

"Oh!" Marissa said. "That's an American expression. Kind of like saying 'I'll be doing two things at once.' I won't be killing any birds."

"I see." Mrs. Nakamura smiled. "You will enjoy watching the wedding procession. You will feel a little sorry for the bride, I think, the wedding attire can be very heavy for them. Fortunately, the weather today is not too warm."

"You know, I'm excited about going to Gion this morning. Thank you for the advice."

. The muted screech of several people pushing back chairs came from the long table. The members of the wedding party stood and the volume of the male voices increased. Marissa leaned toward Ms. Nakamura. "Sounds like the groom's wedding party is getting ready to leave."

The father and his son led a procession of sorts, as the group left the breakfast area. Takeshi caught Marissa's eye and nodded. She returned the gesture.

Mrs. Nakamura leaned forward. "Yes, I'm sure you'll have an interesting day."

***

It had rained a little overnight. The sidewalks in front of the ryokan were still wet in the cracks between the stones. The weather required a light jacket, but the sunlight was bright and the air did not feel humid. If the bride's costume required many layers, the weather could be ideal, as Mrs. Nakamura had suggested. Plus, the cherry blossoms were beginning to bloom. The wedding date was probably selected for the natural beauty of the blossoms gracing the background of the shrine. In spite of their beauty, the thought of cherry blossoms brought a hint of unwelcome panic to Marissa.

She headed for the train station and boarded the train for Gion. She didn't need to consult the schedule. *I've become familiar with the local trains, in just a few short days*. She wondered how the wedding party would proceed to the shrine. Surely, not on the train!

She walked into Gion just as the shopkeepers were

opening their stalls. School children passed in uniforms. One merchant hauled crates of fruit and lettuce into his store. A woman swept the pavement in front of her shop. The business day in Gion was beginning.

There was a canal at the back of the street, with bridges spanning it. Willows lined both banks. The area looked similar to the water next to the temple in her memory, but the expanse of the canal was too wide. Marissa doubted the temple she was seeking was located in the area of Gion, but she could be mistaken. She would try and learn something from the locals and circle back to the Yasaka shrine courtyard from time to time, watching for the wedding procession.

First, though, she wanted to locate Yasaka. After passing the shops and the business area, the courtyard in front of the shrine came into view. The plaza was large compared to other shrines Marissa had seen in Kyoto, featuring a massive orange-red gate, or torii, near its center. Rows of orange- red markers of some type were at the sides of the shrine building. There were several dozen of them, they reminded Marissa of the menu stands at an old-fashioned drive-in restaurant. After walking around the perimeter of the shrine, she found a small tea house on an adjacent street. She ordered a cup of matcha, the brightly-colored green tea, usually served a little foamy. Brent had called it a "gentle green tea cappuccino." She smiled at the thought. Funny, how the return to this location had resulted in recovered memories of Brent that could have remained buried forever.

The shop owner bowed when she asked for the tea. A young woman appeared from the back of the counter, possibly his daughter. She poured the green tea into a large bowl and whipped it with a delicate brush. Marissa bowed as she received the warm bowl from the girl's hands and took it to a small table.

Marissa guessed she was in Gion earlier than the average tourist. A few Japanese men drank their green *Ocha* at a nearby table and two of them stared stealthily in her direction. She smiled and nodded to them before taking out her folding map. The Gion area was easy to find and Marissa looked for the starred locations she'd marked earlier. She planned a route to check out the smaller temples in the neighborhood while she finished her tea.

Marissa walked back toward Yasaka first to see if the wedding procession had started. Conversation buzzed among the few people clustered near the edge of the central courtyard. A tall woman in the group pointed toward a building just to the west of the shrine. A young woman in an ivory kimono and large, rounded headdress appeared, accompanied by a man wearing a dark kimono-like set of garments that implied formality. Marissa wondered if the bride was wearing a wig, because the thick, dark hair was wound many different directions in a style that seemed traditional. Both the bride and groom walked tentatively in the platformed sandals, or *geta*, with their thong-type socks. Marissa guessed they weren't familiar with walking in the footwear, both minced along with shortened steps. A photographer approached the courtyard and directed the bride and groom to assume a couple of poses. The young people wore understated expressions, no toothy smiles for this wedding couple. Marissa did recognize the young man from the ryokan's breakfast area, but his serious expression was radically different from the grin she'd seen earlier.

After the photographer moved his equipment to the side, a line began to form. Two men wearing shorter white robes over colored ones took their places ahead of the bride and groom. Marissa assumed they were priests. Traditionally attired people of various ages lined up behind the couple. Marissa could pick out Takeshi, and she assumed the others were also relatives of the bride or groom. A woman who could be the bride's mother, occupied a space near the head of the line, to the left of the bride. A man dressed in white robes took his position directly behind the bridal couple and held a red parasol over their heads.

 Two musicians carrying flute-like instruments also approached the procession and began playing a tune that struck Marissa as high-pitched and slightly out of tune, but also mysterious and strangely elegant. The priests at the head of the line and the bridal party members began to move forward at a solemn pace. The procession advanced into the main building of the shrine. Marissa could still see a few of the family members from the back, but the bride and groom were hidden from view. She assumed the ceremony had begun. The onlookers began to disperse. She retreated to a bench and took her map out of her tote.

A group of uniformed school children approached. One boy was half a head taller than the rest. He stopped by her bench. "You are looking for something, yes? Maybe I will help."

Marissa looked up into a face that was probably fourteen years old. "Well, yes, I am looking for something. A temple, to be exact. I'm trying to find a place I remember from a long time ago, but I don't know the name of it. All I know is – it is a temple, there is a little pond or canal near it with a bridge, and there is a large cherry tree nearby."

The boy shook his head. "Not knowing the name. That could make it difficult to find."

"Yes, I'm afraid it is difficult. Do you live in Kyoto?"

"Yes, I have always lived here."

The other children were starting to move down the narrow street. "Do you need to stay with your friends?"

Marissa asked.

"I can take a minute," the boy answered.

"Okay, then. Let me show you a picture." Marissa put the map aside and showed the young man the picture Brent had taken of the two of them together, with the cherry tree in the background.

"I see," the boy said. "The temple is not in the photo. May I hold it?"

"Of course. And yes, the temple itself is not in the photo. It was in front of us. We wanted the cherry tree behind us. That is the reason I'm struggling to find the temple itself." Marissa sighed. "What is your name?"

"My name is very long. But people call me Yo."

"Well, Yo, this picture was taken just before you were born, most likely. You can see the large cherry tree here, and the side of a building with some red and green on it. Of course, that courtyard could look different now."

"Maybe. The cherry tree could have died. But Japanese are very traditional, especially in the older parts of cities like Kyoto. So, probably not much has changed. Can you tell me other things you remember?"

"Yes. I know there was water nearby, a circular pond. But not as wide or as deep as the canal running through

Gion. There was a bridge across it, too. I think the bridge was red."

"I see." Yo handed the photo back to Marissa. "There is a large shrine not too far from here, it is famous. There are many garden areas. Travelers visit it every year, from Japan and everywhere. It is called *Heian*. It has many cherry trees, also sweet plum. Is it okay to see your map?"

"Of course." Marissa handed it to Yo.

He pointed to one of the dots on the right side of the map. "It is here. Maybe you will stop by and look. You may have visited it before."

"I will go and find out. I didn't think this search would be so difficult. Until I returned recently, I didn't realize how many temples there were in Kyoto."

"Yes, there are hundreds in this city. May be best to search by pictures first. That might save time."

"You're right about that. Especially since I have only a few days to find the place. I have been looking at pictures online."

"*Un*." Yo made a soft sound that sounded like a polite grunt. Marissa had heard the syllable often in casual conversations she'd overheard recently. She supposed it was the Japanese equivalent of "Yeah."

"Yo, I'm going to take your advice and do a little searching on the internet tonight. But right now, I have another question. Is there an ATM around here?"

Yo looked puzzled. "ATM? Oh yes, you need some yen?"

"I have a little money, but if there's an ATM around here I maybe get some information about a credit card I have."

"Ah. You probably don't have a bank in Japan. Best place to go is in the Kyoto post office. Near the mall and train station. Not far from Kyoto Tower."

"Thanks, Yo. I am going to follow your advice and look at Heian today. I'm a little worried about you right now, though. Won't you get separated from your group?"

"No. We have plan to meet back here in twenty minutes. No problem."

"Well, thank you for your suggestion." Marissa folded her map. "You look a little older than the rest of the students. Are you a special helper?"

The boy smiled. "No. I am a student in first year of high school. But I am a year older than most of the students in my grade. I missed a year of school, because I was very sick."

"Oh. I am so sorry that you were sick. But it seems that

you are well now."

"Yes, my illness has not returned. The doctors check for it two times every year. I had cancer in my blood, very sick for a while. But I was healed with medicine."

"I am so glad for you."

The boy looked at the ground for just a second. "Thank you. Little cost."

"Excuse me? I don't think I understand what you mean."

The boy looked at Marissa's face. "Missing one year of school is little cost. Little cost to get healthy."

Tears stung Marissa's eyes. *This boy sounds like such an old soul.* "My name is Marissa. I am so happy that we had a chance to talk, Yo."

"Thank you. I am glad to meet you, Mrs. Marissa."

"You're welcome." Marissa hesitated for just a moment before continuing. "You see, my husband was also sick for a long time. I know how hard that is." She cleared her throat. "You speak English very well."

Yo grinned. "When I was sick, I watched many movies in English. I decided that would help me learn it."

"I think your plan worked. I have a question for you, Yo. I may make a trip to that shrine you just told me about. But, is there a good cherry blossom watching place near here?"

"*Hai*. Yes, there is one. Just go …" He stood and pointed down an adjacent street. "Turn one corner. You'll see a place where people sit under the falling blossoms."

Two small boys and a taller girl ran up to the bench. "Yo!" one of the boys called. "*Hayaku!*"

"*Chotto matte*." Yo stood. "I need to go now, Mrs. Marissa. I hope you have luck."

"Arigato. Oh, I think you dropped something." A folded piece of bright orange paper had fallen out of Yo's backpack.

Yo looked at the ground. "Oh! One of the cranes I made." He straightened the paper with his fingers and Marissa could see the shape of wings and the head with its pointed beak. "Here, please take it." He held out the origami figure.

Marissa took the folded bird gently by one wing. "Thank you, Yo. I hope you enjoy high school. You appear to be a fast learner." Yo gave her a little bow. Marissa returned the gesture before turning to follow Yo's suggested route. She walked along the lane he'd indicated, hoping that she'd choose the correct corner to turn.

She didn't need to worry. At the next intersection, she looked to her right, and saw an area where cherry trees were evenly spaced with tables arranged underneath them. Most of the tables were occupied, and almost all the people seated at them sipped tea. The trees above them sported a few blooms. The number of buds yielding blossoms would probably increase dramatically by the end of the day, as more of them popped open in the warm sunlight. The sky above was bright blue. A few petals fell and sifted their way to the ground. Marissa felt sure that she would remember how to find this location. She'd try to return in a couple of days, when the blossoms would likely be raining down on the tea drinkers.

A rickshaw stopped on the opposite corner. An elderly man and a younger woman, perhaps his daughter, shared the single seat. The woman stepped out first and assisted the man to unfold his stiff limbs and step down carefully. She put an arm around him and provided assistance as he shuffled toward an empty table. His progress was slow, but steady. He positioned himself in front of one of the seats and lowered himself onto it. After he was safely seated, the woman moved to the opposite side of the table and sat across from him. Marissa wondered if they were participating in an annual tradition. A woman in a kimono approached them and there was a brief interchange among the three. Marissa assumed the older man and younger woman were ordering tea. The tableau in front of her portrayed respect and concern, as had Yo's interaction with her just a few moments ago. Marissa felt enveloped in the cocoon of warmth, respect and gratitude displayed in human interaction.

Should she go to the shrine that Yo had described? She didn't think it was likely to be the one that she and Brent had visited so long ago, but something in the picture she'd showed to Yo had struck a chord of recognition with him. Due to Heian's size, there were likely multiple picturesque spots among the landscaping. Hopefully, she'd find one with a red and green building in the background.

Marissa stood and looked down the narrow street. Wheels had been set in motion in the course of her life. She thought of the monk and his raking in the gravel. *Where am I in this day, this place in space and time?* She had thought of her return to Kyoto as an homage to the past. She was coming to realize, though, that her own life was still in motion, moving toward a future that was uniquely her own. Whether she found the special temple or not, she could never really revisit the cherry blossom temple of her history again. Even in a traditional city like Kyoto, the passage of time was relentless. Change wasn't necessarily good or bad, it just *was*. Her own life journey continued without Brent. Mrs. Nakamura, Takeshi, and even Yo were shaping her life in a different direction. If she had faith in the process, it would work out.

Marissa returned to the bench where she and Yo had conversed less than a half hour before. She opened her map again and looked at the location of the shrine Yo had suggested. It appeared to be close to her current location. She'd check out Heian, and possibly visit the nearby *Konkai Komyo-ji* if there was time.

She stood and began walking north.

CHAPTER ELEVEN: BEFORE

Marissa sat side-by-side with Brent in the boxy exam room chairs. They held hands awkwardly over the armrests, not speaking. Marissa thought the décor represented some designer's attempt to create a sensation of calm, the room gave off a peaceful ambiance with its tones of blue and off-white. A tropical beach scene was framed near the door. A bulletin board occupied the wall to their left, pinned with announcements about support groups and parking instructions for the surgery department.

Brent took in a deep breath and sighed. Marissa squeezed his hand. Noise intruded on the silence as the door flew open and Dr. Copeland entered, shuffling his feet and pulling a chair from the desk. He carried a laptop and placed it on a small rolling table before shaking hands with Brent, then Marissa. "Good to see you," he said, gazing at them over his glasses. "Let me pull up your test results. I looked over them last night."

He sat on the chair and pressed a few buttons on the

laptop. "Yes, here we go."

Marissa looked over at Brent. He was gazing at Dr. Copeland with a serious, unblinking expression. Marissa had seen the look before; Brent was making an effort to hide his anxiety.

"Well, the news is concerning, but not hopeless," Dr. Copeland began. "Your type of testicular cancer is somewhat unusual in a man of your age, and it's one of the more aggressive ones. That's the bad news. There's some good news, though. According to your scan, the cancer doesn't look like it's spread beyond the one testicle. And your tumor also contains cells of a less virulent type, which sometimes slows the growth of the aggressive cells."

Marissa felt her heart sink, but Brent's expression melted into a subtle smile. "I realize that's not the best report. But I feel hopeful."

Dr. Copeland nodded. "There *is* room for hope. Definitely." He swung away from the computer and looked at them directly. His hair was tousled, and he continued to look over his bifocals, reminding Marissa of a mad scientist.

"Well, you're probably wondering about the next step. We're going to refer you to a surgeon. He'll outline your options as far as the surgery goes. Then, after your surgery and post-op testing, you'll come back to me and we'll talk about your chemotherapy options."

"Do I have to have chemo?" Brent asked, his worry on full display.

"Everything is up to you, of course." Dr. Copeland leaned one elbow on the rolling table. "But, even if the surgery goes extremely well and all your lymph nodes are clear, we might still want to consider chemo. It could increase the odds of annihilating any wandering cancer cells."

"I see." Brent looked at the floor.

Dr. Copeland stood. "Well, I'll have your referral documents ready at the checkout desk. Do you have any questions?" He looked at Brent.

It's a good thing he's not looking at me, Marissa thought. *Do I have any questions? Only about a couple hundred of them. But here's the most important one: Will my husband live or die?*

"No," Brent said. "I may have some later, but most of them will be related to the surgery."

"Very good." Dr. Copeland stood and turned to face the door. "I'll be seeing you again."

Very good. Very good! You're telling me that my husband has cancer and you're saying it's very good. Marissa wanted to scream. But Dr. Copeland was out of the room. Brent wore a calm expression; a meltdown on her part would not be helpful. She grabbed his hand again and brought it up to her cheek. "We'll get through this. Like Dr. Copeland said, there's plenty of room for hope."

"I was honest when I said I felt hopeful. I do. I'll fight this thing. And we may even be able to have a baby or two, after all of the therapies are done."

"We'll see. I can be happy with or without a baby. But I can't be happy without you."

They collected Brent's referral papers and left the office. A woman with a walker and a young couple shared the elevator with them. The twenty-somethings exchanged looks like they were sharing a happy secret. Marissa wondered if they'd been to the obstetrician down the hall.

"Let's stop somewhere for a quick bite," Brent said as they exited the parking garage. "I was so nervous, I didn't eat much breakfast. Now, I'm starving."

"Okay." The plan might give them a chance to relax a little. It had been a tense morning. Marissa looked at her watch. It was a few minutes before noon.

Brent nosed their SUV into a parking spot at a burger and beer joint. A Cubs game was on the TV screen in the bar. The cheerful background music brightened

Marissa's mood. After a bite of her favorite chicken-and-Swiss sandwich, she could summon up a little optimism.

"Marissa." Brent got her attention after taking a bite of his giant burger. "There's something I need to talk to you about."

Marissa put her sandwich down. "Okay?" She was aware, after she said it, she'd put her single word as a question. *How bad can this be?*

"I do think I can beat this cancer, and Dr. Copeland agrees, I guess. But there's something you need to know."

"I'm listening."

"Well, about a year ago, my dad's business took a turn for the worse, I guess you'd say. He was bought out by another company, even though he's still CEO and retains a certain percentage of the company's shares, which he'll never part with. But his net worth has taken a hit."

"Meaning….?"

"Meaning my inheritance may not be as big as I once thought. And, after all – it's my dad's money not mine, so I really don't even have a right to worry about it. And if my dad dies before me, well, I will get something. But if I die first…"

"Don't even say such a thing!"

"But I need to say it. If I die first, I hope my dad gives you my share of the estate. But, he doesn't have to, legally. And I don't know how he would feel about it. I haven't mentioned anything to him about my health, because I wanted more information first. Now, I have the information. So, I'll speak to him."

"I don't like talking this way." Marissa struggled to keep a tremor out of her voice.

"No one does. But I just want to be upfront with you. That's all I'm going to say about it for now. It's been on my mind."

"Okay." Marissa struggled to tuck the information into a corner of her brain where she could retrieve it later. In the past, Brent's dad's situation seemed only indirectly related to their own. Now, she appreciated how it could affect her, too.

Brent grabbed her hand. "That stuff was bothering me. I needed to unload it. Sorry if it upset you, but I think I needed to get it off my chest to focus on getting well."

Marissa hadn't thought of that. Brent's comment made sense. She took a deep breath. She'd cry later, if she felt she needed to. Now, she needed to focus on the present. Brent was sitting in front of her, and until he'd made his announcement, they'd been enjoying their lunch. She resolved to get back to that.

Brent focused on the screens around them, updating himself on displayed baseball and football scores. That was Brent, the essence of Brent. So was his concern about her. And his honesty, his transparency. She was truly blessed.

As his eyes darted from screen to screen, Marissa had a moment to reflect on their encounter with Dr. Copeland. He had a reputation as the best oncologist in the area, but he appeared uncomfortable with emotions. The only acknowledgment she'd personally received from him was a limp shake of the hand. Cancer was an emotional illness, so why had he chosen oncology? He seemed anxious to get out of the room, before any emotion was expressed. He even delivered his parting remarks while facing away from them. Brent was probably his ideal patient, concerned but not overtly worried, and expressing hope. Yes, Brent could be Dr. Copeland's poster child.

"Penny for your thoughts." Brent grabbed her hand and massaged it gently.

Marissa chewed the bite of ciabatta in her mouth and washed it down with iced tea. "Just thinking about your oncologist. He seemed uncomfortable with emotion. It was like he couldn't wait to bolt from the room."

Brent sat back in his chair. "Maybe. But I think he's

more the left-brained type. You know, focused on the science and the challenge ahead. And the urge to get out of the room? That might have been the need to move to the next patient. You saw how busy the waiting room was. He has a lot of patients, undoubtedly."

"Yes, you could be right."

"Besides, we did all the research, and he's one of the best. I don't care about his bedside manner as much as I care about his professional reputation."

"You've got another point there." Marissa took one bite of a French fry before pushing her plate away. "Ugh. I'm so full."

"Me, too. But everything tasted so good. I feel much better now. You ready to go?"

"Yep. Leaves are falling at home. They're calling my name."

"I'll help. I feel good, I have plenty of energy now that I've eaten something."

"Great! It's a beautiful day to be outside."

Brent followed through. They spend a couple of hours in the backyard, raking and mulching leaves with the lawn mower. A bank of clouds rolled in, threatening rain. They used a tarp to cover up the one pile they didn't get to mulch or bag. Large drops began to fall just as they put their rakes in the shed.

"Should I make some coffee?" Marissa asked as they went through the back door to the family room.

"Sounds good to me." Brent sat at one of the counter stools. "Tell you what, let me get about forty winks. Wake me up if I start sawing logs. I don't want to sleep through dinner. Or the evening news."

"No worries. I'll wake you." Marissa ground up a few beans and started the coffee maker. Brent stretched out on the couch. His frame was so long that his right leg was angled to the floor, but he was comfortable, evidently. Marissa heard soft snoring when the coffee finished brewing.

She poured herself a cup and went into the small room she'd converted to a study. Originally, it had been a laundry room, but they'd bought a stacking pair of machines and put them in an area once used as a mud room. The repurposing had given her an eight by ten space that held a desk, one small but comfy chair, and a bookcase. Sometimes she used the space to grade her students' papers, but frequently she used it as a reading retreat. As Brent went through surgery and possibly chemo, she may use it as a place to regroup for a few minutes while remaining within earshot. In fact, today might be the first of many times she used the space for that purpose.

She put her coffee on the desk and sat in the comfy chair. She had a perfect view of the front yard and the suburban sidewalk. Children were walking home from school. The mailman was working his way down the street. All of it looked so ordinary. It would be so easy to deny Brent's illness.

She'd never thought too much about what she'd do if Brent was not around. She had her faculty position and her own retirement plan. She could support herself. And she would have the house. If she needed to, she could sell it and move into a smaller space.

She found herself shaking her head. Her perspective had changed in just a short time. What seemed so important a few months ago was not important any longer.

She heard soft footsteps. Brent appeared at her office doorway in his stockinged feet.

"Is there dinner on the agenda for tonight? I think I worked up an appetite in the yard."

Marissa turned in her chair to face him. *I want to hold on to the ordinary for as long as I can.* "What sounds better, spaghetti or a chicken and vegetable stir-fry?"

"Spaghetti, of course! Who can feel down when they're eating spaghetti?"

Marissa sprung up from her chair. "Spaghetti it is." She

wrapped her arms around Brent's waist and gave him a squeeze. "I'll start the water boiling."

CHAPTER TWELVE: JAPAN, DAY FIVE, AFTERNOON

Marissa walked briskly along the route dictated by her phone. *Thank goodness for GPS and walking route directions!* Although she couldn't see any evidence of a temple, she felt certain Heian was only a short distance ahead. A quartet of English-speaking people sauntered about a half block ahead of her. Two American couples traveling together, Marissa guessed. The group took up the width of the sidewalk, and a few Japanese people coming up behind them needed to strategize in order to pass. The Americans seemed oblivious to the obstacle they presented.

Ordinarily, Marissa would have greeted them, but she had her agenda, and time was precious. After passing the group, she could see a huge red orange torii ahead, with a walled enclosure beyond it. As she approached the torii, she could see the shrine itself was set far back from the entrance, beyond an expansive white courtyard. Memories of the place began to jump across the synapses in her brain. Yo had been correct, she *did* come to this place with Brent. Marissa felt her heart jump when she noticed the shrine itself was red and green. Could it be the background structure of her photo? Her pace increased as she moved into the courtyard.

She picked up a pictorial map of the grounds. The gardens were huge compared to those surrounding most temples in Kyoto. Even though the captions on the map were Japanese, the style of the illustrations reminded her of a guide to Disneyland. Yo had hinted at the multiple photo opportunities within the shrine's walls.

She bypassed the shrine itself and oriented herself to the layout of the gardens. There was a lot of ground to cover. *I don't need to scan every square inch.* She'd seek out those places where the red and green roof of the shrine would appear in the background. She retrieved the honeymoon photo from her tote and studied it. The water visible in the picture was slightly to Brent's right, cherry blossoms littered the foreground, and the flash of red and green color filled in the spaces among tree branches in the background. It was difficult to identify a component of a physical structure from the areas of red and green color, though. She couldn't pick out any line suggesting a roof contour or a wall. *I guess my brain had always assumed the red-and-green spot was a roof or overhang. But now that I look at it carefully, I'm not so sure. It's kind of blurry.*

Marissa sat on a stone bench adjacent to the garden path. She spread the map flat on its seat and laid her photo beside it. She found five potential locations where the configuration of trees and water could be a match for her photo. Two of them looked like much better candidates compared to the other three, at least on paper. She marked all of them with her pencil and set off in search of the one closest to the shrine. Based on the illustrated map, it looked to be the most promising.

She walked to the midpoint of the expansive courtyard and found the door leading to the east garden. After passing to the other side of the wall, she couldn't help but gasp. The vista in front of her was one of the most stunning that she'd encountered. The ponds were blue and lovely and pink-blossomed cherry trees lined the walkway to her left, while trees with white flowers were clustered across the water. She followed the path to a point on the opposite side of the pool, where the shoreline's contour made a subtle curve. Standing in the arc would result in water being to her right, with views of cherry blossoms on both sides of the pond, and details of the red-and-green shrine in the background.

The location didn't strike Marissa as a dead ringer for her photo, but she took a couple of photos, including one selfie. She'd do a more detailed comparison once back in her room.

Marissa continued along the same path, then moved farther away from the entrance to the second location she'd marked. Standing with water to her side, she aimed her phone toward the shrine and snapped a picture. She stepped into the shade and viewed the photo, her heart sinking a little as she studied the image. She had to acknowledge the lurking sensation that had sneaked up on her at the first location: Heian couldn't be the site of her quest. The proportions were all wrong, the gardens around Heian were too large, the scale between the water in the foreground and the red-and-green structure in the background was just too great.

She'd examine the spots on the other side of the courtyard. Her map suggested the problem of distance between the structures could be even more apparent from the west side of the garden.

She plopped onto a bench under a cherry tree. Disappointment tried to cloud her brain, but the chaos was tempered by a tiny glimmer of satisfaction. She *had* come to this place with Brent, and she *did* recognize it. The tiny spark of hope would not give in to the confusion of her anxiety. She'd hang onto that spark and persevere until she found the exact spot.

She stood and followed the winding pathways. The grounds were a visual delight at every turn and she guessed she was there at the absolute pinnacle of beauty of the pink-hued cherry blossoms. As she was ready to leave the east garden and cross the courtyard to the west, the four Americans passed through the gate toward her. She nodded but didn't slow her pace. They spoke with animation punctuated by laughter. Marissa wanted to preserve the quiet, focused sensation she'd been enjoying.

The opposite side of the garden contained the pond with the famous stepping-stones featured in *Lost in Translation*. She'd watched the movie with Brent, and he'd commented on their honeymoon experience of hopping their way over the disjointed path. She picked her way over the round stones projecting from the water.

A narrow side trail caught Marissa's attention. She could hear the rhythmic gurgling of running water. The musical sound was coming from a small stream, evidently feeding into the larger waterways of the more formal parts of the garden. Marissa wondered if she was approaching the boundary of the shrine's grounds. The trees grew slightly closer together, and she had to duck to avoid a few low-hanging branches.

After walking about ten meters, she found herself in a clearing, just big enough for two people to stand. A cherry tree stood on each side of the stream. She captured the view on her cell phone screen and compared it to her picture. Definitely not a match, due to the change in the size and shape of the cherry trees.

There was no pond, only a narrow brook. But she'd found a spot for personal reflection. She backed up slightly and looked through her cell phone view finder again and snapped a picture. She felt her shoulders relax, some of the tension left her body. She'd been experiencing beauty, well thought out, with minute attention to color and spacing. Subtle sounds of bird calls and bubbly water overtook the gentle rumble of city noises. All lovely, and she felt guilty for rejecting each one in turn, because they were not the object of her search. But they were her here-and-now. She resolved to notice, and not ignore or reject.

After circling back to the central courtyard, she passed through the shrine's main building on her way out. She joined a steady stream of foot traffic leaving Heian, while only a few people were entering. Marissa planned to take the train back to the station closest to the ryokan, expecting it to be packed with tourists and locals.

"Excuse me, miss, haven't I seen you somewhere before?"

Marissa turned to see a masculine American face, wild red hair, and a beard. The features looked familiar. She glanced down to the shoes; red high-top sneakers. "Oh, yes. I think we met at Nijo Castle."

"Yes, that's right. Looks like we're making the rounds of the same tourist spots."

"We might be." Marissa felt guarded. Not that the guy looked dangerous. She felt exhausted after leaving the temple grounds and didn't want to go into the details of her story. She *was* a tourist, after all. But a tourist with a mission.

"Name's Jeff. Jeff Strange. Yes, that's my real name, unfortunately." He gestured toward the three Asian men directly in front of him. "These guys are showing me around. We're here for a couple of days from Tokyo."

"I see. I came specifically to see sights in Kyoto this trip. But I've been to Tokyo before."

"You sound like an experienced world traveler."

"Appearances can be deceiving." The train station was just ahead. Marissa slowed her pace, creating more distance between them. "Nice to meet you."

"Wait! But I haven't met *you* yet. What's your name?"

"Marissa. Marissa Shively." She turned away from the group with a small wave. "Have a nice afternoon."

"You, too!" Jeff waved with animation as Marissa retreated toward the train station.

Marissa's emotions billowed into a dark cloud as she boarded the train toward Hanamono Station. *I still need to find the temple in my photo*. Yo had some wisdom in his comments. She needed to see *Heian* to rule it out, if for no other reason. There were multiple landscaped sites and cherry trees that she needed to carefully investigate. She'd gone over the likely areas of Heian with care, experiencing some captivating landscapes during the peak of cherry blossom season. She'd completely forgotten about touring the nearby Konkai Komyo-ji, though! She checked the Konkai Komyo-ji website on her phone, only a half hour until closing time. *Too late to return there today*. Marissa sighed, hoping to control her rising sense of frustration.

Helen's wedding was only a few days away.

CHAPTER THIRTEEN: BEFORE

Marissa scanned the surgery waiting area. She felt Helen's gentle pressure on her hand.

"It will probably be a while yet," Helen said softly. "Operations take time, you know."

"Yeah, I know." Marissa turned to face her friend and returned the squeeze. "Thanks for being here. I'm kind of surprised that Brent's dad hasn't shown up." She sighed. "I have to admit, though, I'm relieved. I've interacted with Brent's father very little in our years of marriage. Sitting here with him…it would have been awkward."

"His absence does seem strange. I mean, Brent's one of his two children, and he has a serious condition. And the dad doesn't show up? That is weird."

"Yeah." Marissa shrugged. "Brent says little about his father. I don't know how much he's shared with him about the cancer."

Helen sat with her in silence for ten minutes, before standing and slinging her bag over her shoulder. "I have to head out to teach, but I think your surgeon is looking for you." She nodded toward the double doors where a tall man in green scrubs was removing his surgical mask.

Marissa stood and gave her friend a quick hug. "Thanks again for coming. I'll update you later." She waved at Dr. Osborne as Helen walked toward the exit.

"Mrs. Shively, good to see you." Marissa felt some of her tension release at the warm tone of the surgeon's voice, the relaxed nature of his smile. "Brent did very well during the procedure. Of course, he's been a healthy man most of his life, and that helps a lot. I removed the right testicle and didn't touch the left, as he requested. I also removed a few lymph nodes. They looked fine from what I could tell, but we'll have to wait on the lab analysis to let us know for sure. That will take a week or two."

 Marissa glanced down at the floor before looking into his face. "Thank you, Dr. Osborne. When can I see him?"

"Have a seat for another forty minutes. The recovery room nurse will come looking for you when Brent's vital signs are stable and he's ready to head for the surgical unit. They'll let you know his room number at that time."

Marissa tried in vain to watch the waiting room's television. A nurse walked into the area after a news story ended. She reported Brent was on his way to room 312D and gave directions to a specific bank of elevators. Marissa walked into Brent's private room less than two minutes later.

Brent's facial muscles appeared relaxed. His features looked peaceful. Marissa was relieved to see no hint of a frown or grimace. Still, she felt apprehensive at seeing him so immobile. She reminded herself his surgeon smiled when he'd come to the waiting room to give her his report, and Brent's color looked very natural. He opened his eyes and grinned at her, but quickly drifted off again.

A few minutes passed. Brent groaned a little. His eyes opened.

The deep, throaty noise made Marissa jump. Groaning was unusual, coming from Brent. "Are you okay?"

"Yeah. Just having a little pain. Is it after four PM? I think I can ask for some medication."

Marissa ran her fingers over Brent's forehead, pushing his hair back. "You're keeping track of the time? I'm impressed. It's almost four o'clock now, so let's call the nurse. I'm sure by the time your medicine is ready, it will be time for a dose." Marissa pressed the call button that was anchored to the side of the bed.

"Hello." A stocky, solid-looking man with a shock of black hair and a tan complexion entered the room. He wore green scrubs and had a stethoscope around his neck. "Mr. and Mrs. Shively, I'm Aaron, your nurse. How can I help you?"

Brent cleared his throat. "I need pain medicine, my incision hurts. When I move and cough it's really painful."

"Of course. You have some medicine ordered and I'll get it set up ASAP. But first let me help you get into a more comfortable position. That might help, too." Aaron bent over the bed and helped Brent slide up in one smooth motion. Aaron makes it look so easy, Marissa thought. *I wonder if I could learn to do that so well. Hopefully, I won't need to.*

Aaron stepped out from the room and returned with a giant syringe and some tubing. "I'm going to set up this medication on a pump. Once we have it going, you can give yourself a boost of pain medication whenever you need it. And don't worry, you can't give yourself too much. It has a lockout feature to prevent overdoses."

It took about five minutes to set up the pump. Once it was operational, Brent gave himself a dose of the narcotic. "Hmm. Definitely takes the edge off. But it also makes me a little sleepy".

"Don't worry about that," Aaron said. "Sleep is best for

you for the next 24 hours. I'll be checking on you until seven, and then we'll both talk to your night nurse."

Brent's eyes were closed. "Sounds good."

Aaron smiled before directing his attention to Marissa. "How are you, Mrs. Shively?" he asked. "Surgery can be just as hard on the family."

Marissa fought back tears. "You've got that right. I'm feeling better now that I've heard Brent speak. He sounds like his old self, only weaker and more tired."

Aaron nodded. "He's a courageous guy. I'm going to check on my other patients but call me if you need anything." He patted the pager at his belt. "Just call the number written on the white board, there." He nodded toward the area at the foot of Brent's bed. "Mrs. Shively? Have you had anything to eat today?"

The question surprised Marissa. "Well, only the granola bar I brought with me this morning."

"I'm going to have Theresa pay you a visit. Do you drink coffee?"

"I do."

"Okay. We'll get some to you soon." Aaron left, after dimming the light over Brent's bed. The afternoon sky was darkening, it was getting more difficult to see the cars parked in the lot outside the window.

Brent's eyes closed and his breathing became deep and even. Marissa felt her knotted muscles loosen. She sat in the vinyl recliner to the right of Brent's bed. The surgery had gone well, Brent was recovering as expected, and he needed rest. Marissa realized she was hungry, and her eyelids felt heavy.

"Mrs. Shively?" A young woman in flowered scrubs had entered Brent's room. She carried a plastic tray.

"Yes, that's me. You must be Theresa."

"I am. I'm one of the nutrition aides on the unit. I brought you a snack. And some coffee. Do you take cream or sugar?"

"Just cream. I think I've been so on edge today that I didn't even think about eating."

Theresa smiled. "I hear that a lot. We're here for the patient *and* the family, so if you ever need a bite to eat, just tell Brent's nurse and we'll bring you something." She put the tray on the bedside table and wheeled it toward the recliner.

A turkey sandwich, a mug of coffee, and a serving of fruit in a plastic container were attractively arranged on the tray. The coffee's aroma suggested it was freshly brewed.

"Thank you." Marissa said. "Now that I have food in front of me, my stomach is rumbling." She was tempted by the aroma of fresh coffee but waited until Theresa was in the hallway before biting into the sandwich. The bread was fresh with a crisp crust, the cheese and turkey were savory. She downed the sandwich in a few bites before sipping on the hot coffee. She polished off everything within ten minutes.

Marissa pushed the bedside table aside and flipped on the TV, turning down the audio. Hard to believe it was evening news time. Brent continued to sleep, but Marissa felt oddly comforted by doing something that was part of their usual routine. She didn't focus on the content of the broadcast but enjoyed the pattern of the familiar voices and faces from the TV screen. She noticed the cotton blanket folded on the recliner's back. *This must be here for a reason.* She unfolded it clumsily and threw it over her legs. Her eyelids started to close. She'd only slept a few hours the previous night.

A tap-tap on the door frame got Marissa's attention. Brent seemed to hear it too, his eyelids flickered but remained closed. A tall woman wearing her thick, dark hair in a ponytail pushed a blood pressure machine on a pole. She was accompanied by a petite redhead. They wore matching royal blue scrubs. Aaron followed them into the room.

"Coming in to say good night," Aaron said as he gave Marissa a wave. "I've given these two the lowdown about you, and I'll see you in the morning."

"I'm Annie," the taller woman said as she parked the machine on its pole near Brent's bedside. "This is Dora." She nodded at her shorter companion, who waved.

"I'm Brent's nurse for the night," Annie said as she took out a small notebook from her pocket. "Aaron told me Brent just came out of surgery earlier this afternoon."

"That's right." Marissa nodded.

"Well, I'll have my eyes on him at least every hour tonight, and Dora will be in off and on, too. We'll be taking his blood pressure frequently this first night, also monitoring his IV and giving him several antibiotics. All standard procedure after surgery."

Brent opened his eyes and scanned the room until he found Marissa. His face relaxed when his eyes met hers.

"Annie and Dora are the overnight crew," Marissa said.

"Yes, you're stuck with us tonight." Annie reached for Brent's arm and applied the blood pressure cuff. Marissa heard the machine give its mechanical groan before producing a series of clicks. "One-ten over seventy-four," Annie announced. "Not bad, not bad at all."

Annie turned her attention to Marissa. "We welcome families to stay, but that's your call. Staying all night has its plusses and minuses. The recliner you're sitting on folds out. I encourage you to go home and sleep in your own bed, if possible. We'll be in and out frequently throughout the night. I'll call you around ten this evening with an update, and immediately if anything changes."

"Please go home, Marissa." Brent's voice was soft, but distinct. "You'll sleep better, and I'll see you in the morning. You'll be more alert when Dr. Richter comes around that way."

Marissa hadn't brought as much as a toothbrush with her, let alone a case for her contact lenses or a change of clothes. "I may do that. I'll stay just a little longer, and then head for home. I'll probably be back early. I know you're in good hands."

"How's your pain level?" Annie asked Brent.

"Not too bad. Definitely improved since I took the dose from my friend here." Brent waved a hand toward the pump. "I'll probably sleep well tonight."

"I'll bet you will." Annie wheeled the blood pressure machine near the door. "I'll be back in a little while."

"Thank you." Marissa nodded toward Annie and moved to stand at the head of Brent's bed.

Dora checked a few drawers and restocked items from a cart in the hallway. "I'll be back soon, too. Call me if you need me."

"Looks like we're alone. For the moment." Marissa said as she took Brent's hand.

"Yep. Too bad I'm tied down here." He gestured with the arm containing his IV.

"Be honest. How are you really feeling?"

"Pretty good. Some pain, if I move my right leg. But not unbearable."

Marissa bent down and kissed his forehead.

"Am I Sleeping Beauty?" Brent asked.

"You look beautiful to me. I'm so glad the surgery is over."

"Me, too. But I think I need to sleep now."

"I can take a hint. I'll be back to see you tomorrow morning."

"I'll be more awake then. See you."

"See you." Marissa kissed his forehead again before walking out the door. Somehow, she located her car in the parking garage and drove from the hospital campus to their driveway. She fumbled with her keys before entering her front door. Her fingers found the light switch; the amber-colored walls of the foyer tried to look warm and comforting. But long shadows trailed down the hallway beyond.

CHAPTER FOURTEEN: JAPAN, DAY FIVE, LATE AFTERNOON

Marissa stopped by the Seven-Eleven nearest the monastery park and picked up two onigiri and a salad. She fought to keep her tears of frustration in check while she paid for her dinner. The Cherry Blossom Temple location was elusive, nothing she'd done so far had succeeded in helping her find it. She thought back to Takeshi's raised eyebrows at their curry dinner together, when she'd declared that her heart would lead her to the temple of her honeymoon. Obviously, her heart didn't have a sense of direction, and her head seemed addled as well. All her searching, on foot and online, had not produced a return to the spot she sought. There were still temples to investigate, though. Still some hope.

The clerk smiled as he handed her purchases over the counter. She struggled to return his pleasant expression, hoping her smile appeared genuine. "Arigato gozaimasu." She left the store. Only a few blocks until she reached the ryokan.

A few cherry blossoms landed on the sidewalk in front of her. A reminder that time was marching on. She shook her head at the irony.

Once inside the traditional inn's entry, she set her tote and purchases down in order to remove her jacket.

"Marissa-san!"

Marissa looked up to see Mrs. Nakamura. She was impeccably dressed, as always. Her makeup was flawless, and she wore her signature strand of luminous pearls. She carried a large shopping bag.

Marissa felt her mood lighten a little. "Have you been shopping for clothes?"

Mrs. Nakamura smiled and even laughed a little. "Yes, Shopping is – what is the American expression? One of my guilty pleasures during a trip to Kyoto. If you have time, you should try it."

If I have time… Marissa felt her burst of cheerfulness explode and disappear. Without warning, tears streamed down her face.

"Oh, no. Please forgive me…" Mrs. Nakamura's face reflected concern, even despair.

Great. Now, I've upset her. A double breach of Japanese etiquette, crying in front of Mrs. Nakamura and now upsetting her to boot. Marissa took a deep breath and willed her tears to stop.

"I'm okay," she said with a steady voice. "I just had a frustrating day. I still haven't found the temple, and my time is running out. I will need to leave Japan soon. And more cherry blossoms are falling every day. I wonder if I will even recognize the place if I do find it."

"Come." Mrs. Nakamura gestured toward the table in the courtyard. "Let us have tea. I have an idea."

Marissa nodded and followed her, taking a seat at the table Mrs. Nakamura indicated. Out of the corner of her eye, she noted a subtle gesture between Mrs. Nakamura and Aoi, who was staffing the reception area. Mrs. Nakamura took a seat, settling her shopping bag at her side. Marissa found a tissue in her purse and dabbed at her eyes.

"I have ordered some tea for us," Mrs. Nakamura began. "I am sorry that you haven't found the temple you are searching for. But I have a plan."

"I'm open to suggestions," Marissa said. "My own strategies haven't worked, that's for sure." She focused on the single lily in the table's slim vase to avoid crying again.

Aoi appeared with a lime green teapot and two cups. Mrs. Nakamura nodded, Aoi bowed and left their table.

Mrs. Nakamura poured Marissa a cup of the green tea

before filling her own cup and taking a sip. "My son-in-law has a brother who is a tour guide, here in Kyoto. I am wondering if he could help you. Is it all right if I ask my son-in-law to contact his brother for you? I don't want to interfere unless I have your permission."

"That would be wonderful." Marissa began to feel more optimistic. "I'm assuming the tour guide speaks English."

"Perfect English." Mrs. Nakamura took another sip of her tea. "About half of his tours are conducted in English."

"I would like to meet him. But my time is limited. Can he meet with me soon?"

"If you can be flexible with time of day, and place, I think he could. I'm going to my daughter's home this evening. I will ask."

"Thank you, Mrs. Nakamura." Marissa felt the tension in her neck and shoulders relax as she drank the warm tea. "Arigato gozaimasu."

Mrs. Nakamura poured more tea for Marissa. "I'm confident this can be arranged. Now, why don't you tell me a little about your friend's wedding? What dress will you wear?"

***

Marissa felt better after she returned to her room. In some ways, she felt like she'd had a good cry, but only a few tears had been shed. She placed her Seven-Eleven dinner on the dresser, sat on the edge of the futon, and flopped back. She planned to email Helen after resting a bit. Yes, the wedding was close, only a few days away. And she needed to work on that toast. Telling Mrs. Nakamura about her role in the festivities increased Marissa's enthusiasm.

She pictured herself wearing the lavender gown hanging in her closet at home. She had to admit it flattered her figure and complexion, plus it was dignified-looking and stylish at the same time. It would be fun to devote a little attention to her appearance for once. And if some miracle happened, and the temple was found soon, maybe she could spend a little time shopping in Kyoto. Mrs. Nakamura's advice could probably help her to maximize her time in the shopping district.

She picked up her salad, found the plastic fork in the Seven-Eleven bag, and started to eat. The vegetables were crisp and the dressing provided an interesting flavor. Maybe things would work out. The son-in-law's brother could be the key person to help her. She thought of a few phrases to incorporate in her wedding reception toast and jotted down ideas in her tiny pocket notebook.

Munching on the crunchy salad whetted her appetite. She ate one of the rice balls before opening her computer, saving one for later. Time to email Helen and work on some final plans concerning Helen's reception. Hard to believe that the events were only a few days away.

She thought of Takeshi as she typed in her computer password. Would she see him again? She hoped so, but now that his nephew's wedding was over, he probably wouldn't be in Kyoto much longer. She played through a scene in her mind, where she'd tell Takeshi she'd found the special temple and he'd say…something. Something profound with a Japanese flavor. Like a line ending a movie. Fade out. Sentimental music. Happily ever after.

She opened her email account. A message from Helen appeared near the top of her Inbox, as well as one from Sandy, Helen's matron of honor.

Helen's email was short. Two brief paragraphs summarized her bachelorette party. She ended with wedding festivity details.

I hope you won't be too jet lagged when you get back. The rehearsal will be at 6:00 at our church. If you don't want to attend that, I do understand. But the rehearsal dinner will be a good opportunity for you to meet the people you don't know in the wedding party. And Chad's family members, of course. I know you'll like

153

them.

Marissa expected to like Helen's fiancé's family, based on the stories Helen had told her. She felt some of her apprehension and resistance to the event lift. *Now, if I can just find the cherry blossom temple, I'll feel like I can move on, and concentrate on Helen's wedding. It's hard to feel festive while I'm anxious about finding it in the time I have left.*

Marissa made herself stand up and walk across the room to her tote. She rummaged around for her larger notebook and turned to a blank page toward the back. She consulted the smaller page where she'd written the few notes. She wanted to focus on Helen's friendship, her role in bringing her together with Brent, and more recently, her devotion in staying by her side during the last hours of Brent's surgery and keeping in contact with her through the difficult times. But, how to do that without bursting into tears? Maybe the easier thing would have been to stand at the altar with her friend. At least, she wouldn't have to say anything, and a few tears would be expected.

Too late now. She was committed to the toast and the matron of honor was thrilled to relinquish that task. Her email said she was "petrified of public speaking".

Focusing on glowing generalities could be one way to handle the toast. Helen would know exactly what she meant by her references and that was the important thing. She sat down with her larger notebook and jotted down a couple of paragraphs. Surely a few minutes' worth of comments would be plenty. The attendees would look forward to the end of the toast, because then it would be time to party in earnest.

Marissa read what she'd written and made a few changes. She was reasonably happy with the result, although it still needed some fine-tuning. She'd make a computer document a little later and continue to work on editing the toast, some minor tweaking. It would be finished in a few days, now that she had a draft to work with.

She started an email to Helen.

I'm getting excited about your wedding and the toast is coming along. I just have a little more editing to do on it, and it will be ready to go. Of course, I'll be at the rehearsal dinner, wouldn't miss it!

Sounds like you had fun at the bachelorette party. At about the time you were cavorting with your wedding attendants, I was at a marriage ceremony on the other side of the world. I discreetly took a few pictures, and when you're back from your honeymoon, I'll show them to you after we get done looking through your wedding photos. I think you'll enjoy seeing the traditional Japanese wedding garb, quite different from Western styles. I've heard some Japanese brides will wear the traditional costume for the ceremony but switch to a modern dress for the reception.

More later, Marissa.

She logged off and closed the lid of her laptop. *Things were looking up.* She glanced at her cell phone and noted it was only a little after seven o'clock. Too early to turn in for the night, and she didn't want to work on the toast anymore. She thought of returning to Gion. Why not? She might be able to see a geisha or two. Evidently, they were easiest to spot after dark.

She tossed a sweater over her white blouse and brushed her hair, fastening it into a ponytail at the nape of her neck. She freshened her blush and lipstick before grabbing her tote and retracing her route to the train station.

CHAPTER FIFTEEN: JAPAN, DAY FIVE, EVENING

A different pace resonated through Gion at night. The foot traffic bustled, people moved rapidly in opposite directions, and an undercurrent of conversation and laughter comprised its soundtrack. Marissa headed to the area noted for its teahouses, taverns and geishas. She found a bench near a busy corner, out of the stream of traffic, but with a view of two cross streets. A black car turned the corner and came to a stop. Two kimono-clad women wearing geisha make-up exited the back seat and quickly entered a tea house. *Now I see how their faces appear after dark. Not as garish as I was expecting.* Both women wore their hair in the traditional upswept manner accented with sparkling ornaments. The kimonos' detailed embroidery caught the streetlights too, adding to the illusion of glamor. *These women stand out in a crowd. They contrast with the Western idea of beauty, though.*

Two slim men in business suits approached the teahouse on foot. One appeared to be in his thirties, while the other looked to be a generation older. The older man appeared to be telling a joke. He gestured dramatically with his hands. Marissa wondered if he was more than a little drunk. After the pair entered the tea house, the street traffic slowed, but clusters of people continued to amble by. Their conversation was punctuated by laughter, but there was no shouting or rudeness.

A larger party of men, about ten in all, rounded the corner. They were dressed in traditional costume. One young woman accompanied them, and to Marissa's eyes, she looked similar to a geisha, but something was different. Her obi was tied in a flowing bow for one thing. Marissa inhaled sharply when she recognized one of the men as Takeshi, grateful that her bench was shadowed from the streetlights. The group progressed down the street, and all entered a courtyard about ten meters from where she sat.

Marissa felt her heart race. Why was a single, very young-looking woman, accompanying all of these men? Takeshi was a Japanese man and he was doing what Japanese men do, evidently. She decided to leave the area. If the group passed the bench again, she didn't want to be there. She'd feel like a spy.

She found the place where she'd met Yo and followed the streets to the tea café under the cherry trees, the same place she'd watched the older man and the younger woman drink tea earlier in the day. There was no tea service now, but some of the tables were occupied by young adults. They sat in couples and small groups, mostly on the seats, but a few sat on tabletops. Some held bottles that they brought to their lips at intervals. This area was quieter compared to the Gion street she'd just left. If she knew Japanese, Marissa would be able to understand some of the conversation around her. She heard intermittent words and phrases, punctuated by periods of silence. There was a very faint breeze, and she could see the occasional cherry blossom make its descent in the dim light.

She took a seat at one of the tables on the outskirts of the area. A few of the young people cast a glance her way. There was enough light for them to see she was not Japanese. A few hushed comments sounded like questions. Maybe they thought she was waiting for someone. Maybe they thought she'd been stood up. The rhythm of the conversation returned to its former level within a couple of minutes. She'd become part of the background. Marissa was almost glad she couldn't understand the whispered words she overheard from time to time; she found their rhythm soothing.

A cherry blossom landed on the table surface directly in front of her. It was perfect, no petals had been lost on its journey from the tree. Marissa thought of taking it with her. *I can't. It's too delicate.* She felt as fragile as the blossom. *This is where I am in this space in time. Alone, in a quiet café, in the moonlight. In Japan. Watching rituals of life here, all around me. When will I rejoin the stream? I feel like I'm watching life instead of living it.*

Marissa began to retrace her steps. She turned two street corners and reached the main thoroughfare, one that would take her to the train station. She made her way on the extreme edge of the road, trying to avoid stepping on toes. Most of the pedestrian traffic was headed in the opposite direction. A group of men in traditional garb stood out in the crowd approaching her. No geishas accompanied them. Takeshi was visible for a second, then he was lost among a sea of bobbing faces. A few seconds later, Marissa felt a soft warmth on her forearm. Then a firm hand cupped her elbow. Gentle pressure guided her to the side of the road where she turned to face Takeshi. She took a deep breath. She hadn't had physical contact with any Japanese people since her arrival in Japan.

"Marissa." Takeshi released her arm. "Sorry to be so abrupt. I wanted to talk with you."

"You surprised me."

"I'm sorry if I startled you. I wasn't sure if you saw me. I wanted to make sure you didn't get swallowed up in the crowd."

Marissa nodded. Her emotions had already been fighting within her, now Takeshi's sudden move to change her course spun everything into a new direction. She needed a minute to adjust.

"Let us find a teahouse and sit down," Takeshi suggested. He looked away, scouting the nearby businesses. He waved at the other men in his party, as if telling them to go on.

He's giving me a chance to compose myself. Marissa inhaled and exhaled slowly.

"Ah. An excellent place just a minute's walk away. They serve the highest grade of tea, including some rare ones for this area." Takeshi pointed at a narrow storefront with a sign overhanging the narrow street, before glancing at Marissa. "My company supplies them." Takeshi's understated boast hit its mark, Marissa felt her shoulders relax. She couldn't resist smiling.

The owner's eyebrows raised when Takeshi walked through the narrow doorway, and his expression quickly became anxious. Takeshi's appearance there must be a big deal, Marissa thought, like a visit by a celebrity.

They took seats at a lacquered square table. Takeshi gestured toward the owner, who wore a worried expression.

"Marissa-san, I wonder if you are upset. Perhaps your search for the temple is not going well?"

Marissa sighed. "You are right. I met a young student today who gave me a little hope. I followed his suggestion and spent a lot of time going to a place that was very beautiful and had some of the features that I remembered." She shook her head and looked at her folded hands on the table. "But it was not the right place."

"Ah. I see. Frustrating."

"Yes." Marissa looked at Takeshi's face. "But the temple and its grounds were peaceful and calming. I am glad I saw it. And I do see many sites around Kyoto that remind me of Brent. Things he said. Things I didn't even know were in my memory. But, thanks to this trip, I am remembering these experiences, which is a wonderful and unexpected gift. Maybe those memories are the important thing, not so much finding a particular patch of ground, or a certain stream or pool. After all, water is water."

"You sound very wise."

"I do?"

"You are learning lessons that life is teaching you. That is wisdom."

"Sounds so simple."

"Many people never learn it, though."

The teahouse owner arrived with the tea in a heavy-looking metal pot with an ornate handle. "This tea is called *Gyokuro*," Takeshi said. "It is grown in only one place, a small hillside near Uji, and harvested by human hands. I think its unique flavor gives wisdom and strength to those who drink it."

"I think I need both right now." Marissa resisted the urge to put her head in her hands. Takeshi's words about her wisdom surprised her. *Maybe the journey to wisdom is sometimes painful.*

Takeshi lifted the sturdy pot and filled her cup, then gestured with an open palm toward his own. Marissa lifted the pot by its handle. "This kettle is heavy."

"It is. It will keep the tea warm for a long time."

Marissa wondered if his comment meant their conversation would take a while. Did Takeshi's remark indicate a hint of interest in her? Her heart fluttered in her chest.

Takeshi patted his jacket pocket. "I bought this for you, after my nephew's wedding. While we were still at the shrine." Takeshi brought out a square brocade object with a gathered drawstring at its neck. It was slightly puffed up, like it contained something. It reminded Marissa of a tiny gift bag. He placed it in her hand.

She ran her fingers over the smooth fabric. "Do I open it?" she asked.

"I am glad you asked. No, you should not open it. The little pouch itself is the gift. It is a type of good-luck token. This one is specifically for luck in searching for something. The luck lasts for one year."

"So it's a good-luck ticking time bomb?" Marissa tried to lighten the mood, but she regretted the words instantly. Would Takeshi take them as an insult?

She exhaled when Takeshi burst into laughter. "Not a time bomb, surely. More like an extended hourglass."

"Or falling cherry blossoms." Marissa said.

"I guess you could use that example. But, unlike the cherry blossoms, this good luck does last a year. Remember that. And it is a good thing that you did not open it. That would have let the good luck escape."

"Oh. I'm glad I resisted the temptation, then. I have enough problems as it is."

Marissa sipped the tea. It tasted like green tea, but the brew had a light brown hue. It tasted very smooth and a little grainy. "This is delightful. I will miss the excellent Japanese tea when I get home." She took a deep breath. "I want to ask you something."

"Of course."

"I decided to come down to Gion, to see if I could catch sight of a geisha. I did see several. And I saw you with one of them, I think."

"That could be. I did visit several teahouses. A *maiko* was with me part of the time. She is a geisha-in-training. She is sister to the groom, my niece."

"Your niece is going to become a geisha? How does her family feel about that?"

"Why not? This is Kyoto, the center of the geisha world."

Marissa decided to be blunt. "Well, aren't geishas paid by their male companions...for whatever..."

Takeshi set down his cup. His tranquil expression morphed into a suggestion of surprise. She'd seen the same expression on his face only once, when she'd told him that she'd find the cherry blossom temple because her heart would lead her there.

Takeshi cleared his throat. "Some Westerners think that geishas are prostitutes, probably due to the so-called "geisha-girls" who appeared after World War II. They were definitely not geisha, who are more like hostesses or companions for an evening, or maybe just an hour or two. They are keepers of an historical part of Japanese culture. But the relationship with a geisha is social and cultural, nothing more."

"It just seems strange. You would rather pay for someone to accompany you than ask someone you know?" Marissa blushed. Her comment sounded rather forward, especially in the understated Japanese culture.

"This part of Japanese life may be very strange to the American way of thinking. Probably even antiquated. And the geisha way of life is dying, slowly. There are fewer geisha now. In a hundred years, there may be none."

"What is the attraction? For their male customers, I mean."

"Well, in Japan, marriage for the woman usually means being a house-wife, more or less literally. Married women usually stick to the home, their job is to run it with efficiency. The husband turns over most of his salary to her for running of the household. Their social life outside the home is usually with members of the same sex, unless it is a family gathering."

"So, how does that fit with the geisha world?"

"Well, Japanese men enjoy a night out with a beautiful woman representing the best of Japanese culture. Especially if they are in Kyoto, the capital of the geisha world."

"Hmmm. Just seems strange from my point of view. In America, much of our social life takes place with the spouse. Many married couples have a date night several times a month. Your mate is supposed to be your romantic interest."

"Well, that is interesting, but just different to how traditional roles are viewed in Japan. But, since I am a life-long bachelor, maybe I am not the best person to be describing Japanese marriage."

Marissa didn't know how to respond. Date nights had been something to look forward to when Brent was healthy. She couldn't speak for all American couples, though.

She tried to smile, hoping she looked nonchalant. "Something to think about. But the house-wife thing, I find that idea repellant. I'm surprised a modern woman would stand for that."

Takeshi merely shrugged and poured her more tea. *He seems so much more spontaneous, and his speech is more Western. In some ways, I feel like we're becoming good friends.*

"Your turn." Takeshi said.

"My turn for what?" Marissa brought herself back to the present.

"Your turn to say something."

"Oh! My mind went off on a tangent. Thank you for

bringing me back to the present."

"Any time. I'm happy to be of service."

Marissa laughed.

"I think that is the first time I have heard you laugh," Takeshi observed. "At least, laugh in that way."

"I was thinking the same thing about you. Just a minute ago. You have a nice laugh."

"Yours is very musical."

"Oh!" Marissa drained her cup. "I don't think anyone has ever described my laugh before." She paused. *Now what do I say?* "Thank you for the tea. I've enjoyed talking with you. I think I will take the train back to the ryokan. I have a big day tomorrow, my time for searching is getting short. Soon, I'll need to pack up and take the train back to Tokyo and the airport."

"I will walk with you as far as the train station. I need to meet my brother before I go back to the ryokan, myself."

Takeshi bowed to the shop owner. Marissa watched the man behind the counter let out a pent-up breath. *Looks like he's relieved to see us go.*

The pedestrian traffic had thinned. They sauntered along the Shirakawa River with its overhanging willows. The air smelled fresh and floral.

"The moon is especially beautiful tonight," Takeshi said.

Marissa stopped walking and looked up into the dark sky. The moon was waxing; somewhere between half and full. A halo of white light surrounded it. Both the moon and its halo were reflected in the quiet waters of the Shirakawa. "It is pretty. With the willows, the water – and the way it is reflected…"

"Yes."

They walked the last block to the train station in silence. Marissa stopped at the stairway leading to the platform. "Thank you for walking with me."

Takeshi turned to face her and bowed slightly. Marissa returned his gesture before she turned away from him and descended the stairs.

The train was only half full and Marissa easily found a seat. She settled into its gentle rocking rhythm as it pulled away from the station. She found herself reviewing the evening's events in her mind, especially her conversation with Takeshi. Her eyes were closing from time to time. She recognized what she was doing, although she hadn't experienced this ritual for almost two decades. Her reminiscence of her encounter with Takeshi was a first date feeling! This constant reviewing and savoring every gesture and word…she'd done that before. But not since her first date with Brent.

She opened her tote and removed the amulet Takeshi had given her, tracing the design in its fabric. Takeshi had been sensitive to her mood. His behavior showed empathy, a trait she highly valued. Well, she had to admit, it could also mean he was an excellent salesman, very attuned to the subtle behaviors of his customers. Didn't he even tell her that, at their first meeting? "I see the world as a businessman." Something like that. Was he working on closing any type of deal with her? She felt like laughing out loud at the thought, but she controlled herself. The Japanese people around her would probably think she was crazy or drunk.

Her mood quickly sobered when she thought of how short her time in Japan was becoming. Would something happen tomorrow in her quest for the temple? If not, she would have to accept that fate could be taking her in a different direction. Takeshi had hinted her insight was wisdom.

Marissa wasn't so sure.

***

A faint tap came from the hallway. Was someone knocking at her door, or was it just an incidental noise from an adjacent room?

"Marissa-san." A hushed female voice came from the hall.

Marissa slid open the door connecting her anteroom with the hallway. "Mrs. Nakamura! Good evening."

"Good evening. My son-in-law's brother will meet with you tomorrow. If you can be at the Gion Shijo Station at noon, he can talk with you for about thirty minutes. The tour clients will be given some time to explore on their own at that time.

"I would be happy to meet with him. I'm familiar with the Gion station after being at the wedding, and I just returned from there. Actually, I saw Takeshi in Gion. He told me his niece is a maiko."

"Oh." Mrs. Nakamura nodded and directed her gaze away from Marissa. "It seems your mood is happier now."

"Yes. I'm sorry, earlier I was concentrating on the negative parts of my day. But there were some good things, too. I am frustrated about not finding the temple. I don't know if it matters anymore. Maybe the point is to continue my life's journey."

"You could be right…" Mrs. Nakamura's voice trailed off.

"I did see some beautiful things."

Mrs. Nakamura nodded, and Marissa continued. "I didn't tell you earlier, but I did get a chance to see the wedding procession. It was quite a contrast to the noisy breakfast earlier today. And I met the most amazing boy named Yo. He once had cancer. A courageous young man. He made me think of Brent, my husband."

"Yes." Mrs. Nakamura nodded.

"I saw an old man and his daughter making their way to a table under the cherry trees. So touching, to see the younger woman assisting the older gentleman."

"Yes, the cherry blossoms symbolize the fleeting nature of life. Sometimes people with serious sickness will come and lay on a blanket under the falling flowers."

"I see." Marissa paused. "And later, I saw two geishas get out of a limousine and enter a tea house. And later still, I saw Takeshi with his niece. About an hour after that, I ran into him near the temple where the wedding was held. We went to a tea house together."

"Oh?" Mrs. Nakamura said. Marissa thought she detected a subtle change in her friend's expression. Was Mrs. Nakamura concerned?

"We talked a little about the geisha culture. He said spending time with geisha is a desirable social activity for men, even married men."

"It is true. Many businessmen will take advantage of a

trip to Kyoto to spend some time with a geisha. Perhaps some male relatives of the groom did so tonight."

"Oh. That could be, given what Takeshi told me. At the teahouse, we had a very different kind of conversation. Takeshi sounded almost Western. I felt like I was talking to a friend in an American coffee shop."

"I see." Mrs. Nakamura paused. "Did he also say the moon was especially beautiful tonight?"

Marissa's jaw dropped. "He did! How did you know? Were you in that area tonight? Did you overhear us?"

"It's the typical thing for a Japanese man to say when he's interested in a woman."

"Really!" Marissa's hands flew to her cheeks as they started to burn. "I had no idea."

Mrs. Nakamura smiled. "I thought as much. I wanted to educate you."

"Well, I'm glad you did, I guess. I don't exactly know what to do with that piece of information, though." Marissa looked away for a minute. *Take a deep breath. Focus on something else, at least for the moment.* "Meeting at the Gion Station." Marissa said aloud before writing the phrase in her notebook. "Very good, I will be there tomorrow at noon. What does your son-in-law's brother look like?"

"He is a little on the short side. He wears glasses with black frames. He will be wearing a blue jacket with this emblem on it. May I?" Mrs. Nakamura took Marissa's notebook and pencil and drew the emblem, a triangular crest containing several kanji characters.

"Perfect! I should be able to recognize him. I'm assuming you told him what I look like?"

"Yes. He will be looking for you also. Good night."

"Good night, Mrs. Nakamura. And thank you."

CHAPTER SIXTEEN: BEFORE

Marissa felt an impish urge to mix things up while they waited for Brent's PET scan results. Maybe *she* should perch on the table in Dr. Copeland's exam room. So far, Brent had never sat on the thing. Was there a patient gown around? She could look in the drawers built into the table's side. If she found one, she could put it on and hop up and sit on the table's paper cover. Wouldn't Dr. Copeland be surprised at that! On the other hand, he might not even notice. Some days, she wondered if he was even aware that she was in the room. He barely acknowledged her presence. He never asked for her thoughts. If he didn't have the best oncology reputation in their area, she'd have recommended that Brent fire him long ago.

The door opened and Dr. Copeland appeared. He looked a little less like the mad scientist compared to previous encounters. His hair was neatly combed. He was wearing new glasses and for once, they weren't dangling off the end of his nose. His expression was serious, though, with lips pressed in a firm line. Marissa couldn't recall seeing him with his eyebrows knit so closely before. *This isn't going to be good.*

Dr. Copeland sat directly across from Brent. He pulled up his chair, he and Brent were almost knee to knee. Marissa realized that even the posture Dr. Copeland assumed excluded her.

"The news isn't encouraging," he began. Brent met his gaze, didn't waver, didn't even blink. His expression remained calm, but solemn. Marissa tried to keep her focus on Dr. Copeland's words, but her mind darted elsewhere. She caught a phrase here and there, but possible future scenarios jumped to the foreground of her mind. Did the results of Brent's PET scan mean more surgery? Chemo? Or both? She didn't think radiation therapy was a possibility, but she was far from an expert.

Dr. Copeland droned on, evidently outlining options and the prognosis for each one. She imagined he was also presenting the downside of each treatment, but she couldn't force her brain to pierce through the tone of his voice and construct the meaning of his message. What did the results hold for Brent, and for their marriage? She found her mind projecting several scenarios, none of them good.

She came back to the present when she heard Brent say, "I will." *I will what?*

Dr. Copeland stood and shot Marissa a glance that was probably meant to be sympathetic. He opened the door and left the room.

It took Brent a moment to stand up.

Marissa stood and touched his arm. "I don't know about you, but I found Dr. Copeland's comments overwhelming. I couldn't really keep up, I guess because he talked so fast."

"Well, I only expected him to say one thing," Brent turned to face her.

"What was that?"

"That my cancer was gone. But that didn't happen."

"I gathered that. But how bad is it?"

"Well, he thinks it's bad enough for me to consider chemo. Maybe even more surgery, removing the remaining testicle. But I know those choices are wrong for me."

"What are you going to do, then?"

Brent dropped the mask-like attentive expression. He looked toward the floor before getting his coat off the hook behind the door.

"Let's talk about it once we get outside. We can walk in that little park, just across the road from the emergency room entrance."

The frost they'd seen on the early morning grass had disappeared thanks to the midmorning sun. Brent led the way down a trail carpeted with mulch. A couple of sweet gum trees still held onto a few bright leaves. A pair of cardinals darted among them while squirrels chased one another around the trunk of a giant oak.

"I've been anticipating the news today," Brent began. "Of course, I was hoping for a cure. But I knew I had to at least consider that some cancer remained. Still, it was a shock when Dr. Copeland started talking today.

"I've looked around online since the surgery. Virtually meeting people with the same form of cancer. Talking to them about their treatments and how it made them feel. I told them I wanted their honest assessments."

"And?" Marissa matched the rhythm of Mark's stride.

"I decided I'm not going to pursue any further treatment. I'll let nature take its course."

Marissa stopped walking. Brent took a few slow steps before he realized she wasn't at his side.

"You can't be serious," she said. Tears threatened to sting her eyes. She didn't want to cry in this public space, even though no one was within view. She needed privacy. It was time to head back to the car.

Brent walked back down the trail to face her. "I am. Serious, I mean. I just can't go through that much discomfort if it isn't a cure. I don't want to watch my own life just slip down a drain in slow motion." He grabbed both of her hands, squeezing them.

"I don't think I know you very well." Marissa struggled to keep her voice under control. "I would think you would want to hang onto life at any cost."

"Well, after looking into the options, I decided that the cost could be too high. Or maybe, just too futile. And then there's the quality of life issue. I like a life of high quality. Otherwise, it just isn't worth living."

So spending more time with me isn't quality for you. The tears spilled over her eyelids and dashed down her cheeks. A sob escaped before Marissa could muffle it.

"Hey! Please don't do that. I'm just trying to be brutally honest, and I guess I'm succeeding." Brent wrapped his arm around her and pulled her into the fluffy down pillow of his coat. "I don't feel like I have the luxury of waiting for the right moment. Waiting for any moment."

They walked the rest of the way to the car in silence. Once inside, Marissa looked for her stash of emergency tissues and grabbed a handful. She sobbed uncontrollably. She couldn't remember giving in to this much sorrow since she was in grade school. There was no maternal embrace to comfort her now.

"Please don't. Please don't." Brent kept repeating the phrase over and over. Marissa needed to slow the flow of her tears so she could properly yell at him.

"So, I must accept your emotion. Unconditionally, correct?" Marissa hiccupped as she tried to speak through her sobbing. "Because *you're* the one with cancer. But what about *me*? You're saying that I don't have the same right? I can't express my emotions? You're so full of it!" If they weren't so far from home, and if her eyes were less red, Marissa would have left the car. It would probably be easy to catch a taxi from a hospital's front door. Or maybe she'd just call Helen.

She looked out the car's window, away from Brent, and took a few deep breaths. Driving home would only take ten minutes. She'd calm down enough to make the trip. Then, she might need to isolate herself in her study for a while. Maybe do her own internet searching.

After blowing her nose and wiping the remains of the mascara off her eyelids, she started the ignition. If the parking attendant was shocked at her facial expression as she paid the fee, he didn't show it. *He's probably used to tears and signs of distress, attending a parking lot near an oncology office.*

"I'm sorry." Brent faced her after he unlocked their back door. "Don't be angry with me. I've thought this through. I hoped I wouldn't have to tell you about this decision. I was hoping I wouldn't have to use this plan I've made."

"I know." For a nanosecond Marissa felt calm and in control. "But I never thought about living without you. Not in this decade, anyway." She tossed her coat into the laundry area. "I'm going to spend a little private time in my study. I need some space to think things through and gather some information. Then we can have a discussion. Write down the names of some websites to look at. And put the technical names of the cells in your tumor on the paper, too."

"Okay." Brent went to the kitchen counter, grabbed a pencil, and started scribbling on a pad. Marissa made a mental note to search for spouse support groups, too. Someone had to be out there who understood how *she* felt.

Brent tore off the top sheet and handed her the paper containing the few notes he'd scratched in pencil. "I'm going to chill in the family room. Just watch some sports TV from the couch."

Marissa took the paper and retreated to her study. The volume of the TV was low and she found the muted voice of the sportscaster almost comforting, so she left the door open. She faced the blank screen of her computer before taking a deep breath and signing on. First, she looked for information about the tumor types.

She'd done this once before, had even jotted down a few notes, but hadn't referred to them once since Brent's surgery. *Denial.*

Yes, she knew Brent had a combination tumor, including cells of the worst kind. But the worst kind was usually made less worse by the presence of cells from the least severe type, which were also present in Brent's tumor. However, one website warned the severe type could dominate the tumor and grow rapidly or spread to other parts of the body. She'd look at Brent's chart online in a day or two. Dr. Copeland's notes from today's visit would be posted by then and they should provide insight into what the oncologist was thinking. The PET scan results would be available, too, which would provide information about cancer spread to other parts of the body. *Why didn't I pay more attention while we were at the office?*

Marissa decided to defer looking at specific chemo regimens for the moment. She searched for websites and chat rooms for both cancer patients and their spouses. There were several accounts of the chemotherapy experience both from the patients' and spouses' point of view. Their stories were evenly divided; half were positive and half were negative. Several said they would never choose to go through chemo again.

Marissa pushed her rolling chair back and put her face

in her hands. She remembered the day, early in their marriage, when she and Brent bought life insurance policies. "One of us will exit this life first," Brent had said. "The other will need some financial protection."

So, now she knew. Brent would be first. She would be left, whether Brent had chemo, or not. Maybe her desire for him to have chemo was related to her own fears of being alone. Postponing the separation, the grief. A desire to stay in the cocoon of denial.

Regardless of his treatment choice, she needed to support Brent now. He needed her.

Brent was awake, looking at the TV screen with a calm expression on his face. If he had been asleep, Marissa would have allowed herself to sob without restraint. Instead, she shed a few quiet tears and resolved to call Helen later in the day. Now, she wanted to spend some quality time with her husband.

.

CHAPTER SEVENTEEN: JAPAN, DAY SIX, JUST AFTER MIDNIGHT

Marissa placed her laptop on her closed suitcase and sat cross-legged on the edge of the futon. After typing in the keywords *geisha*, *make-over* and *Kyoto*, she skimmed the ads that came up. There were several pages of advertisements and reviews, but one business announced they catered to customers "aged 6 to 60 years". If they could transform a 60-year-old into a geisha, they surely should be able to do something with her, Marissa thought. After all, she was almost twenty years shy of their upper age limit.

The business was called *Enchanted Time*. In addition to the many still shots of transformed geishas on the border of the webpage, there was a central area with a video depicting one customer's transformation, collapsing a half hour's activities into thirty seconds. The process involved a wig, white foundation makeup, black eyeliner, and very red lipstick applied only to the lower lip. Some rather plain white undergarments were put on, making the customer look like a black-haired ghost. Once the kimono was donned the customer's appearance became much more credible. By the time the obi was added, along with a fan and an ornate hair ornament, the geisha look was complete. Marissa thought the customer's transformation was nothing short of remarkable.

Why not do it? I may never be in Kyoto again. Or, if I am, I may be past 60 years old! The website described a basic package for about $70, including a few photographs and 30 minutes to walk around Kyoto in the costume. The next day's appointments looked full, except for two slots first thing in the morning. She'd take one. After all, she had to wait until almost noon to meet with Mrs. Nakamura's tour guide contact. Her makeover would be fun and would also kill some time until her appointment. She put herself in one of the empty appointment slots. After entering her credit card information, a screen popped up. "Do you want to select your kimono in advance?"

Marissa shrugged. Selecting her kimono now might save her some time. She clicked Yes, and rows of kimonos appeared on the screen. She scrolled through them looking for a garment with a cherry blossom motif. One came into view; pink and white flowers on a light blue background. She chose it, then was directed to a screen that asked for her height. After filling in the blank, she pressed enter, and was faced with a screen that said "We will see you soon" with a cluster of

Japanese characters underneath the English phrase. She was committed. There would be a few pictures as souvenirs. She'd show them to Helen, after her wedding, when Helen would likely regale her with scores of wedding photos.

She could show a photo to Takeshi, too. Marissa felt certain they'd see each other at least one more time. Maybe she'd even give him a picture, as a remembrance. She thought back to their conversation in the teahouse; barriers around them seemed to break down that evening. They were talking as friends, maybe even good friends. She pondered this idea. Well, maybe not good friends yet…but they conversed like people who were on their way to becoming good friends. Or maybe more.

Marissa felt her cheeks burn when she remembered Mrs. Nakamura's interpretation of Takeshi's comment about the moon. Marissa had to admit the idea of Takeshi having interest in her was exciting, but that excitement also seemed a little dangerous. She should not be developing an attachment to someone she wasn't likely to see after she left Japan. Someone so different from herself, but who had some uncanny similarities to Brent, at least his connection to a family business. And those similarities to Brent may not be good things.

She focused on her quest for the Cherry Blossom Temple. She would give it one last try. She fingered

Brent's wedding band on the chain around her neck. If locating the temple didn't happen, she'd have to face that reality. Maybe it just wasn't meant to be. Maybe the life lessons she was learning were the real purpose of the trip. She could accept that. But what would she do with Brent's ring if she didn't find the place? Would she feel okay about leaving it in the place she'd chosen at *Heian* Shrine? *Full circle,* indeed. She felt like she was in a maze, or a dizzying spiral.

She checked her email, no message from Helen. Marissa planned to send her one last note before leaving the hospitality of the ryokan, but she'd wait until tomorrow. She slipped into her Japanese pajamas and stretched out on the futon. The wind had picked up, but its rhythm was steady and Marissa found it almost comforting. She felt safe, secure, and hopeful. The next day should bring sunshine.

***

Parallel lines of light ran across the Hydrangea Room's window shade. Birds chirped and warbled outside, the howling wind of the previous night had been replaced by a gentle breeze. Marissa donned a tank top and a pair of capris before adding a semi-tailored jacket. She'd grab a rice ball or two for breakfast from the Seven-Eleven near the station. She'd slept a little later than she'd intended. *Don't want to be late for my appointments. At least I can skip the makeup routine for now. That will save a few minutes.* She put a few cosmetics in her purse, though. After the geisha makeup was removed, she'd need to apply something before her meeting with Mr. Saito, the brother of Mrs. Nakamura's son-in-law.

She scurried through the courtyard connecting the monasteries. The sunshine enhanced the green of the grass, the gray of the gravel, and the delicate pink of the many cherry blossoms littering the ground. When she exited the gate and passed a cluster of trees with almost-bare branches, she realized the previous night's wind had dislodged many of the cherry blossoms in the area. The experience of sitting under gently falling flowers could be over for this year.

She hoped the wind hadn't been as strong in the Gion area. Marissa made her purchase of onigiri and boarded the train. She'd wait until she arrived at the Gion station before finding a bench and enjoying her breakfast. She hoped to find plenty of cherry trees sporting blossoms once she'd traveled a few miles.

The train was jampacked and she almost didn't reach the its doors to exit at her stop. She tried to make her way up the stairs without plowing over anyone in front of her. When she got to street level, she found her way to the blossom-viewing area that Yo had recommended the previous day. She sighed, there were many more blossoms on the ground compared to those remaining on the trees. A few people enjoyed morning tea at the tables in spite of the almost bare branches above them.

Marissa checked her watch. Twenty minutes until her geisha makeover. She sat on a bench and ate her convenience store breakfast while she surveyed the downed blossoms surrounding her. She felt solemn, but not exactly sad. This state of affairs, cherry blossoms downed by the wind, was a part of life. She had to accept it. Maybe the makeover experience would distract her and get her back into something closer to a cheerful mood. She didn't want to be despondent when she met with the tour guide. After all, Mr. Saito was going out of his way to help her.

She found her way to the geisha makeover business without problem. *I'm not ready to be a tour guide yet, but a few days of hanging around this neighborhood has paid off.* She pushed on a screened door and a bell chimed. A young Japanese woman appeared behind a counter. "Ohayo gozaimasu," she said.

Marissa returned the morning greeting. "Ohayo gozaimasu."

"Is this your name?" The woman behind the counter pointed to Marissa's name on a computer printout.

"Hai." Marissa nodded yes.

"Come." The Japanese woman beckoned with an

exaggerated motion. She was dressed very simply in black slacks and a white shirt. Her ebony hair was pulled into a sleek ponytail. She led Marissa to a room featuring a row of small lockers. "Please." She offered Marissa a laminated instruction sheet with English on one side, Japanese on the other.

"Please to remove your outer garments and shoes and place in locker." Step One read. "We will provide you with traditional undergarment."

Marissa removed her capris and jacket and put them in the locker. She left her tank top on. She quickly took the elastic band she had on her wrist and gathered her hair into a ponytail near the crown of her head.

"Step 2. Put on full-length garment first, then white short garment over your head."

The attendant held out a pink gown that looked like a lightweight robe an American might wear over pajamas. Marissa slipped her arms into the sleeves; the Japanese woman lapped the front and tied it in place with a narrow strip of fabric. Then, Marissa pulled the white, shorter garment over her head.

"Step 3. Put on the *tabi* (socks) then step into slippers provided."

The Japanese woman gestured to a bench, indicating that Marissa should sit. After she was seated, the attendant brought out a basket from a cubbyhole near the lockers. Marissa selected a pair of socks and put them on, noting the division between the big toe and other toes. They felt strange on her feet.

The attendant brought her a pair of plastic slip-on shoes. After Marissa slid her feet into them, the attendant beckoned again and walked Marissa to an area with three swivel chairs in front of mirrors. Once Marissa was seated, the Japanese woman rolled out a cart with a quart sized cup containing a thin paste-like liquid, plus pots of black and red makeup with brushes. A wig occupied a space on a shelf underneath the makeup and application equipment.

The Japanese woman took a white cloth and dampened it with a pleasant-scented liquid. She rubbed the cloth all over Marissa's face, neck, upper chest, and upper back. She took the container of white liquid and held it in her left hand. She looked at Marissa's reflection in the mirror. "First, white base layer," she said. Marissa gave her a subtle nod.

The woman took a brush-type instrument with foam at its tip. The white foundation liquid looked and felt very watery as it was applied to her face, neck, chest and upper back. But after a minute, it began to dry. Marissa was surprised to see her face transform to an oval of opaque, matte white. The attendant fanned her for a few seconds. "Must be all dry," she explained.

She reached for the wig and set it down on Marissa's head, pulling it down by the sides near the temples. Next, the Japanese woman took a small pot of reddish powder and applied a little to Marissa's eyelids, followed by a cream-like black eyeliner applied with a fine brush to both her upper and lower lids. A red cream rouge was added to her cheeks, and another brush was used to apply lacquer-red lipstick to her lips. The lip outline was narrow, unlike the very full lip look popular in the states.

"Only three makeup colors for geisha. White, black, red," her attendant said. "What you think?"

"I'm amazed," Marissa said, looking at her reflection in the mirror. "Hmm. I'm glad I'm going to have photos taken. I don't think I could explain this result in words."

The Japanese woman smiled and nodded. "Almost time for kimono. But first, let me get basket…" She scurried to the closet at the back of the room and selected a floral ornament with strands of dangling spangles. "For your hair," she explained. She took some long hair pins and fastened the ornament, featuring pink cherry blossoms, securely into the rounded contour of the wig. "Now, follow me. Last time."

Marissa obeyed. She was led to a dressing area that looked much more formal than the locker room she'd been in thirty minutes ago. The cherry blossom kimono was waiting for her, along with a pair of shoes and a parasol. Marissa took off the plastic slip-ons she'd been wearing. The attendant motioned for Marissa to step into the geisha shoes, which featured a thong on a platform sole. Marissa thought they resembled little tables.

"*Geta*," the Japanese woman explained and gestured toward the shoes as Marissa tried to slip them on her feet. "Not wear too tight. Leave space." She pointed to the area between the thong of the sandal and the gap in the tabi socks. Marissa nodded. Evidently, she was not to shove her foot into the shoe too much, leave some space between the thong of the shoe and the gap between her toes.

Marissa was directed to hold out her arms, while the attendant helped her into the kimono itself. The garment felt surprisingly heavy. Like the undergarment, the Japanese woman lapped one front panel over the other and tied them in place with a narrow cord. She brought out the pink obi which she centered in front and tied in the back. Tying it took a few minutes, and Marissa couldn't see what was going on. She felt a little antsy while trying to hold perfectly still. The weight of the kimono increased with each second.

"You are ready. Time for first picture."

Marissa twirled a little clumsily in front of a mirror before leaving the dressing room. The shoes were a little awkward, but really – she looked and felt transformed.

She walked into an adjacent room, which was a photo studio of sorts, with different backdrops tacked up to its walls. A photographer lounging in the corner sprang to attention when Marissa entered. He bowed. "You look very beautiful," he said. It sounded like a phrase he'd practiced multiple times. Marissa got the impression he couldn't understand English well. She was tempted to say, "I'll bet you say that to all the girls." But instead, she dropped her eyes and bowed a little, hoping that was more geisha-like.

He pointed to the cherry-blossom backdrop. "This is perfect," he said. The Japanese woman directed her to stand on the two footprints lacquered to the floor. "Look this way," the photographer directed as he began snapping photos. "Now, cheen up. Yes, up." Marissa looked toward the ceiling. "Good, good," the man said as he continued to look through the camera lens. "Now, try garden shot."

Marissa moved to another backdrop and placed her feet over the footprints there. She was facing the opposite direction from the first pose. This time the photographer directed her to aim the parasol in a different direction and look down slightly. Marissa wondered if she was supposed to look demure. After a few shots, he directed her to the "cheen up" posture again and snapped a few more. "Good, good," he said for the second time. "Now, you walk around, yes?"

Marissa remembered seeing this feature in the ad, one half-hour to walk around Gion as a geisha. She was not sure this part of the package was desirable, especially because the platformed geta made walking a challenge. The small, mincing steps that she thought were stereotypical now seemed to have practical value. In fact, that was probably the only way to walk in the lacquered shoes without falling.

"Okay," she said to the photographer and her stylist. "I'll try." The stylist directed her toward a door. It led out to the street and was only about fifteen feet from the door she'd entered through.

A couple of blond girls were approaching the entrance. "Oh, look!" one of them said, pointing in Marissa's direction.

It's like she's in awe of me, Marissa thought. Maybe I make a pretty respectable geisha. She decided to walk to the area with the tables interspersed among the cherry trees. Walking there and back would probably take a half-hour, given her six-inch stride.

Even though most of the blossoms had fallen, people were gathering for tea under the trees. Marissa learned that walking in the *geta* was easier if she relaxed into the shorter steps and walked a little slower. She got a few glances, some from men, some from women. *I*

195

wonder if they think I'm ridiculous, she thought. I suppose some of the Japanese women and girls do the geisha makeover, too. This experience is not only for foreign tourists.

The sky remained cloudless. At least there was a silver lining to the winds of the previous night. The breeze was slight. The air was warm, but not hot. She'd try to make the most of the situation. It would be a good day for sightseeing, possibly the best she'd had since her arrival; certainly better than the day she'd taken the train to Uji.

She approached one of the tables and sat down. Drinking tea would be a socially acceptable reason to sit and give her a break from walking in the geta. A young woman approached her and asked, "Ocha?" Green tea?

"Hai." Marissa replied.

The young woman returned with a small pot and a handleless cup. She poured tea for Marissa and bowed.

"Arigato gozaimasu." Marissa nodded her head and the server retreated. Marissa took a sip. The tea's temperature was perfect for drinking and she enjoyed its delicate flavor. *This Japanese green tea is far superior to what I've tasted at home. I need to enjoy the opportunities I have in front of me. Right now.*

A single cherry blossom floated down and landed on her wrist. A second later, one landed on the surface of her tea. She decided to leave it there, after last night's rain it would be clean. Maybe it would bring her luck.

Marissa shaded her eyes and looked at the branches of the tree above her. They were almost bare, but a few blossoms remained. *Maybe it's not too late.* She sipped at the tea, draining the small cup. The cherry blossom at the bottom was too soggy to save as a souvenir.

Time to mince back to the geisha studio. She didn't want to be late for her appointment with the brother of Mrs. Nakamura's son-in-law.

Marissa removed the kimono and the makeup before dressing in her much lighter Western clothes. She took a few minutes to apply the makeup she'd stashed in her purse. Her stylist took her to a small room where Marissa could view the photos taken a half hour earlier. Marissa's eyes widened when the images flashed on the screen. She looked transformed. They were much more flattering than she would have imagined. Mr. "Cheen Up" was more skilled at photography than she'd given him credit for.

"You paid for two poses," the attendant reminded her.

"Can I buy more?" Marissa wanted to know.

"You could buy all. We put on disk. For 2000 yen.

Worth the price, your pictures turn out beautiful."

"Yes, I want the disk." Marissa picked out the best photo from each background for printing. In five minutes, she received a folder containing the two 5 by 7 photos and the disk containing all the poses. Maybe she'd give one photo to Takeshi. After all, she could make as many copies as she wanted once she got home.

She'd think more about that later. Now, she needed to hurry. Her appointment with the tour guide was only thirty minutes away.

CHAPTER EIGHTEEN: BEFORE

Marissa thought she'd hit rock bottom, the deepest valley of despair, when she'd learned Brent's cancer had returned. Circumstances surely couldn't get any worse. But she was wrong.

The early November sunshine was starting to make its way into their backyard that morning. She'd just poured herself a cup of coffee, and Brent had finished his morning high-protein shake. He'd retreated to his favorite spot, the window seat that faced their back yard. His dramatic weight loss allowed him to fit on its narrow surface with room to spare. The bird feeders, squirrel corn, and various trees attracted colorful birds and small mammals, even the occasional rabbit. Sometimes Brent listened to audio books or tranquil music. On this particular day, though, he was simply observing.

Marissa sat at a small table where she could also see the backyard view. She remembered trying to focus on the moment, enjoying the view of the sparse amber leaves still clinging to the trees. Brent surprised her by sitting up, an action that was difficult for him. He patted the window seat. "We need to talk."

Marissa steeled herself. A discussion about funeral or memorial service details was surely on Brent's mind, or changes to his will. She put her coffee on the table and sat next to him on the thin cushion. She put an arm around his bony shoulders, stifling the urge to wince. The cancer was starving him. His muscular bulk had burned away, used for energy to keep him alive.

Brent took a deep breath and said, "I'm putting the house, and all of our assets, in your name."

Brent's statement was radically different from the scenario Marissa expected. Her muscles froze and it took a moment to find her voice. "What? I can't believe what I'm hearing."

"I can't believe I'm saying it, either. And I don't intend for anything to change between us. But I also feel a strong need to protect you."

"Protect me from what?" Hadn't she already faced the worst-case scenario? Her husband was dying. She couldn't be protected from that.

"I'm talking about the financial aspect of things." Brent stopped and shook his head, like he couldn't believe something. "We need to put all assets in your name for your protection. I don't trust my father or his business associates. You'll have the house, free and clear when I die. That's important for your financial future."

Marissa couldn't think of a response. It sounded like Brent may have been keeping information from her. The idea was as almost as upsetting as his decision to avoid chemo.

"Marissa, in life, I've protected you from my father. His greed. Now I need to protect you after I'm gone. No one needs to know about the legal process except you, me, and my lawyer. Our lives go on together, as long as they can."

Brent planned to move some of their money around, and then put all their assets in her name. It was their money, so they could do whatever they wanted with it. However, she might have to face the wrath of his father alone. Her right hand went to the gold band on her left ring finger. She began twisting it. *Full circle.* Something didn't seem right, in fact, it seemed ironic. This latest plan didn't fit. She had shared everything in life with Brent.

Brent went on to explain some of the family business details. How Marissa could lose the house if they didn't separate their financial assets before his death. He was genuinely concerned, she could see that. But she felt blindsided by the suggested plan and her own emotions: surprise, disgust, even a hint of betrayal. But admiration was there, too. Their marriage had its ups and downs, but she'd always been convinced it was strong. She knew Brent held the same opinion.

The silence was becoming uncomfortable. "What do you think?" Brent asked.

"I don't know what to think. I need some time to process this knowledge. Your father gave us the down payment for this house as a wedding gift."

"Yes. But I'm afraid he may consider that down payment an indicator of ownership now. His latest business dealings have led to losses. After I'm gone, I don't know how he'll behave. I just want to make sure you have the house, free and clear."

"I know." Marissa tightened her arm around his shoulders, horrified anew at the lack of flesh covering the bones. "I do appreciate that you're concerned about me. I love that about you. But give me a little time, okay? Let me process this. At least give me one night."

"Okay." Brent kissed the back of her neck. His kisses were rare now, Marissa had assumed the lack of physical signs of affection was due to the amount of pain he was experiencing, or fatigue, or the effects of the pain meds themselves. Now, she wondered if his lack of touch was related to the secrecy surrounding his father's business. *Secrets never help relationships.* Marissa felt tears seep into her eyes but refused to let them fall. She needed to stay strong in front of Brent and do her crying in private.

She stood, keeping her back to him, just long enough to control her tears. Then she turned around. "Enjoy your bird watching. It's a lovely day. I'm going to retreat to my study for a little bit. I need time to think right now." She walked across the room to her study door and closed it partway. She wanted the suggestion of privacy, but she needed to hear Brent if he needed anything.

Brent was right, his time was getting short. How bad was this financial situation? Anger began to creep into her shoulder and neck muscles. Brent had been hiding aspects of the situation from her for a while now. Maybe the financial concerns were there before his illness. Why hadn't he told her? They'd always said they could get through anything. Suddenly, she desperately wanted the coffee that was still sitting on the table in the family room. She peeked around the door. Brent appeared to be sleeping. She padded across the room in stockinged feet, returning to her desk with mug in hand.

She sat with her cup, looking out the window toward the street and their front porch. Marissa had always liked this house on the quiet cul-de-sac. It wasn't a mansion, but it was bigger than she needed, bigger than they'd needed as a couple. It was comfortable, and they'd lived in it more than a decade, years of memories were integrated throughout the two-story Tudor with its shaded back yard. If it was just a matter of selling the house, she could live with that. She might prefer to move to a different, and smaller place, at some point.

Really, Brent's bombshell was telling her the situation was bigger than the house. Their situation was possibly not too different from those faced by elderly people, when one had extreme dementia and had to be institutionalized. Sometimes the nonimpaired spouse even divorced the other to keep their home. Both she and Brent were in control of their faculties, though. And Brent, the spouse with the illness, was suggesting the plan.

What would happen if they didn't follow through with Brent's suggestion? Brent made it sound like the house might have to be sold to cover business debt. And how much more would she owe…to somebody? She'd been thinking that Brent's father and brother had been distant due to their inability to cope with Brent's illness. Now, she wondered if other factors were involved. Brent had shielded her from all of that. His ability to protect her from family turmoil would end in the next few months. Her emotions ranged from the shock to a warm sense of appreciation, to anger at a father that couldn't be a parent to his son. She felt admiration for Brent's strength and desire to shield her from danger, though that feeling registered as crazy in part of her brain.

Brent did have a lawyer. Maybe she needed her own, but not for the usual reasons. She'd start by consulting the legal expert in her circle of university friends. Things could get complicated, and the complications could linger after Brent's death. She'd need an advocate then. She could accept the practical nature of Brent's proposal, but it left her feeling profoundly sad.

How will these legal problems affect our relationship now?

She and Brent were still a team. She'd take the situation full circle.

CHAPTER NINETEEN: JAPAN, DAY SIX, MIDDAY

Marissa found Mr. Saito easily. He sported a navy blazer with the emblem Mrs. Nakamura had sketched on its breast pocket. His black-framed glasses gave him a serious, professorial demeanor. His eyes scanned the crowd from behind the lenses. Marissa approached him and watched his focus settle on her.

"Shively-sama?" he asked softly.

"Yes, I am Marissa Shively. Please call me Marissa."

Mr. Saito bowed. "Of course. And please call me Tom. That is what I ask my English-speaking clients to call me. It's close enough to my Japanese name." He smiled as if his comment was an inside joke.

"Tom it is, then." If Marissa wasn't focused on devoting every second to her search, she would have asked for his Japanese name. "I appreciate your willingness to meet with me." Marissa dug in her tote for the honeymoon photo. "This is the picture that I've been showing to others, hoping that it will trigger recognition of a location in Kyoto. My husband and I were at a temple at the time, but the direction of the photograph doesn't show the temple itself, unfortunately. We aimed the camera to show the cherry blossoms. What the picture shows is very near the temple, I think. But the process of finding the temple itself is much more difficult than I thought it would be."

"I see." Tom gestured toward the photograph. "May I?"

"Of course." Marissa handed him the photo. "I had been thinking this small red-and-green area in the background was part of a building. But after looking at it closely yesterday, I'm not so sure. It could be something else."

Tom took the photo in both hands and looked at it through his glasses, before shoving the spectacles atop his head and studying the image a second time. "Hmm. Can you tell me what else you may remember? What did you do just before or after taking this photo? That information may help."

Marissa looked away from Tom and tried to gather her thoughts. "I think you're the first person who has asked me that. It's a good question. Let me think just a minute." She wished she'd brought the photos from the entire day's activities to Japan. She'd never thought that the progression of activity may have been helpful, until now. *Too late.*

Tom prompted her. "Did you eat a meal or snack? Buy a souvenir?"

"I think we were at this location toward the end of the afternoon. My husband loved to criss-cross the city. We took the train often. Buses sometimes, too. This may have been our last stop for the day…" Marissa closed her eyes and tried to go back to her stored memories. She and Brent had purchased a few souvenirs, most of them for other people: Helen, her parents, Brent's father and brother. She willed herself to relax, trying to conjure up images from that day fifteen years ago.

A detail came into the edges of her memory. She could remember Brent's madras plaid shirt and her floral print dress, the bright sunshine, the breeze and the cherry blossoms drifting toward the surface of a pond. She opened her eyes. "I remember something! We were running out of time. The souvenir shop at this temple was just about to close. But we bought a little token for my friend Helen. Something that would bring her luck in love." It was a little plaque. Marissa had forgotten the detail until just now. She'd left it in its box, presenting it to Helen on their return. "I think the souvenir was a little card-like thing, or a small plaque. There were two fish on it."

"Hmmm. Okay." Tom nodded and closed his eyes, as if to help him concentrate. "Love tokens are sold in many places in Kyoto. I have another question for you. Are you sure you are looking for a temple?"

Marissa took a moment to respond. "Well, yes. At least I think so. What else would I be looking for?"

"Because there are both temples and shrines in Kyoto. And I wonder if you are looking for a shrine, not a temple."

"Ah!" *Could this simple error have cost me time in finding the place?* "What is the difference?"

"Shrines are Shinto holy places. Temples are Buddhist. Both traditions have had a long presence in Japan, and in Kyoto."

Marissa felt a quiver in her stomach. "I'm so ignorant! Yes, the place I'm looking for could be a shrine, I suppose. I think most people have been suggesting both temples and shrines, even though I've been using the word 'temple'." Marissa tried to contain her anxiety. After all, Yo had sent her to *Heian*, a shrine. "Does that help you think of a place?"

"Maybe. It is…how do you Americans say? A long shot. But something about your picture reminds me of the area near the *Rokusonno* Shrine. I don't know what the red and green area is, but I wonder if it is a sign or something in motion on the street. That area of the photo is a little hazy, while the rest is clear. Rokusonno is very close to streets and businesses. Also, they sell souvenirs at Rokusonno that have carp illustrations. The shrine has a pond, and it is inhabited by koi, the Japanese ornamental carp."

Marissa inhaled sharply. Tom's description was sounding hopeful, but she didn't want to be disappointed. "If Rokusonno is so centrally located, I wonder why no one has mentioned it to me before. According to the map, it looks like a train runs by it."

Tom's lips curved upward in the hint of a smile. "The *shinkansen* tracks are closest to Rokusonno, but those tracks are fairly new. Local trains don't stop in the immediate area. Rokusonno is one of Kyoto's best-kept secrets, some Kyoto residents don't even know about it. It is small, but it does have a pool and a large cherry tree that produces many blossoms. Recently, Rokusonno is being promoted as a place for weddings."

Marissa sighed. "Rokusonno may be a long shot, as you say, but it may be my best hope right now. Can you give me directions from here?"

"My pleasure. The shrine is not too hard to find. Let me see, from here…" Tom looked over his shoulder, as if to get his bearings.

"I have a map. Can you show me?"

Tom took the map and placed an X in Gion with his ballpoint pen. From there he drew a dotted line to the

Rokusonno shrine which was labeled on Marissa's map. "You can walk to the train…" He gave a series of instructions that required another walk, a bus ride, and a final leg on foot in addition to the train. "If Rokusonno is not the place, I would recommend strolling along the Philosopher's Walk. It is easy to find nearby and has several spots that resemble areas in temples and shrines."

Marissa folded the map and pressed it to her chest. "Arigato gozaimasu." She felt like giving Tom a hug but resisted. The gesture would not be welcome, she felt sure. She took two steps backward and made a little bow.

Tom bowed slightly and gave a subtle wave. "Good luck. I hope you find what you are looking for."

Marissa took a few steps before she looked back over her shoulder. "I'll let Mrs. Nakamura know if I find it. You'll get a report from your brother."

***

Rokusonno. The name didn't resonate with any stored in Marissa's memory. Still, she felt her chest warm with a hint of hope. She rounded a corner and leaned against the first building that was out of Tom's line of sight. Hopefully, Tom's hunch would lead her to the right place. She took a few deep breaths, exhaling slowly after each one. One more temple…if this wasn't the temple, or shrine, of her honeymoon, she might experience a meltdown. *Maybe I could leave the ring at Rokusonno, anyway. Or at Heian, because I remember being there with Brent.*

She headed for the Kawaramachi train station. A train arrived within five minutes and she rode to the Omiya South Station only a few minutes away. The Shijoomiya bus stop was only half a block from there. Another five-minute ride and she was walking the last leg, about a kilometer according to her map, but she'd end up at Rokusonno. She felt as if she was being guided. *I'm really getting familiar with Kyoto and its transportation system. Maybe I could live here. I have a sabbatical coming up in two years.* The idea made her feel a little giddy. *Probably wishful thinking. I'm imagining myself in the prelude for that perfect Hollywood ending. But what if it doesn't happen?*

The train track closest to Rokusonno belonged to the *shinkansen*, or bullet train, traveling between cities on its magnetic tracks, not the local train. But still, she only had to walk a few more blocks. Or as they say in Japan, a five minutes' walk. Marissa' lips curved into a smile in spite of her apprehension. *I'm starting to think like the Japanese.*

Compared to the grandeur of Heian Shrine, Rokusonno's dimensions were miniscule. The simple grounds were surrounded by businesses, the shinkansen tracks and secular signs. Marissa approached the gate. A thin man wearing Japanese formal garb turned to face her from the inside of the enclosed area. Marissa had seen his ensemble before, at Takeshi's nephew's wedding. Maybe he was a priest.

His lips formed one word. "No." He may have whispered the word. Marissa wasn't sure if she heard it. But his meaning was clear.

"No?" She said aloud.

"Wedding." The man's voice was hushed and solemn.

The shrine was closed temporarily for a wedding? Would it reopen soon? Marissa typed a message into her online translator. "When can I enter?" She showed the Japanese translation to the priest.

"Maybe tomorrow," the man said in English.

"No." Marissa said the word, then typed frantically on her phone screen. "I need to be in today. My husband and I came here after our wedding. It's very important."

The man read the screen, nodded and held up two fingers and pointed to his wrist. Marissa hoped his gesture meant two o'clock. Marissa nodded, then bowed. It was just before one o'clock. She'd find a place to eat something; her stomach was rumbling. Some rice, vegetables and green tea would be refreshing.

She found a table in a tea house west of the shrine. She ordered a meal with matcha, then watched as the shinkansen glided past on the tracks. Compared to a conventional train, it was so quiet. Amazing. A few children on the sidewalk stopped to watch the bullet train whiz by, the adults seemed to accept it as part of the background. Maybe she'd take the shinkansen from Tokyo to Kyoto during her next trip. She felt certain she would return to Japan. The when was less clear, though. Hopefully, not too many years away. Maybe she could count the time between trips in months, not years.

Marissa sipped her tea leisurely after her plate was cleared away. She took her small notebook out of her tote and worked on Helen's wedding toast. It was almost done, just maybe a minor change here and there and it would be ready. She returned the notebook to her tote before closing her eyes. She could hear Brent's voice describing the geraniums on Japanese sidewalks. She smelled the cotton fabric of the tee shirt he wore on the night they met. Her fingers went to the infinity pendant and his wedding ring, hanging beside it. She could be close to fulfilling her mission, parting with Brent's ring. Marissa sighed before opening her eyes.

She felt the solemn sting of finality, similar to when Brent died, but less intense. She hadn't thought too much about parting with the ring. After a minute, she removed Brent's wedding band from her necklace and placed it on the tabletop in front of her. She positioned it so the *full circle* script faced her and snapped a photo with her cell phone, using the zoom feature. Then she rotated it to get a picture of their wedding date.

A cherry blossom landed next to Brent's ring, before it was whisked away by the spring breeze. The tiny flower was a thing of beauty, but it was delicate and would not last forever.

Her watch read ten minutes till two. She returned the ring to her necklace, tugging on it to make sure she'd closed the clasp completely. She almost jogged back to the Rokusonno Shrine entrance. The priest was only a few feet from its gate. Had he stayed in the area for the hour she'd been gone? He noticed her approach, beckoned to her and opened the gate.

She faced the temple, which was set back from the street. The paved courtyard in front of it bustled with people, wedding guests most likely. Marissa walked to its edge and turned around. She scurried over to the east side, faced the temple, and turned around again. She felt the resonance of familiarity. After taking a deep breath, she walked through the central area of the courtyard to the gardens beyond.

Her heart began to beat faster. A glance at her watch revealed she had several hours until closing, plenty of time to explore every nook and cranny of the small temple area if she needed to. The cherry trees in one corner seemed to be at the end of their budding phase, multiple blossoms were open and only a few had started to fall. Maybe her luck was changing. At least, these trees hadn't been ravaged by the winds of the night before. A stone bridge spanned the narrowed strait of a pond ahead of her. The railings on its side were constructed of wood, painted red. A cherry tree with a large canopy was just a few feet from the shore at the far side of the bridge. Some of the blossoms were raining down on the water, but half of the pond's surface was visible, unlike that day so many years ago when the surface was littered with petals.

A large, flat rock adjoined the path in front of Marissa. She walked over to it and sat down, placing her tote beside her. She reached to the back of her neck and unclasped her infinity symbol necklace. After placing it in her lap, she removed Brent's wedding ring from the chain. She carefully fastened the necklace again, giving it a gentle tug before standing up. She would be heartbroken if she ever lost Brent's wedding gift. His gold band felt warm and smooth in her left hand as she stood.

Marissa walked over the bridge and stopped at its highest point. She dropped the gold circlet into the water, watched a pair of orange-and-black koi dodge its descent, and saw it come to rest between two mossy rocks on the pool's bottom. She looked around the area, turning in place to take in a 360-degree view. She placed her hand over her heart and concentrated on the spots of sunshine dodging the tree branches and the gentle whispers created by the breeze. She'd imagined a feeling of exuberant joy at this moment. Instead, she felt calm. A feeling of peace rippled from her heart and spread through her limbs. She turned and retraced her route to the more central part of the garden.

A wedding party and a photographer were making their way to the bridge. The chain of events was fitting. She made a brief stop in the gift shop, bought a wedding amulet for Helen and a small plaque with the double koi motif for herself.

It was time to take the train back to the ryokan. Hopefully, Takeshi would be there when she got back. She couldn't wait to tell him about her good fortune.

***

Sweat trickled between Marissa's shoulder blades as she trudged up the incline from the train station to the ryokan. She set down her tote to remove the jacket she was wearing over her sleeveless top.

A black sedan turned the corner ahead, proceeding in her direction. A back window rolled down as the vehicle approached. "Marissa-san!"

 Marissa looked up to see Takeshi extending his hand out of the rear passenger window, palm facing her. The car slowed its pace as it passed but didn't stop.

"Takeshi!" Marissa raised her hand in greeting. She watched the vehicle turn another corner before she hoisted her tote over her shoulder. She'd freshen up and change clothes after she returned to her room. Packing for her return trip was a priority, but she hoped Takeshi could share in the success of her afternoon at some point that evening. She'd leave a message for him through the ryokan receptionist. Maybe the gesture was a little forward by Japanese standards, but her time was short.

Her mood became one of pleasant anticipation. Was it due to finding the temple, or more correctly, the shrine? Or maybe her feelings were related to her anticipation of recounting the afternoon's events with Takeshi? Or maybe a little of both. No matter, she needed to get back to the ryokan, leave the message, and start getting organized for her trip home.

Aoi greeted her from behind the lectern in the reception area. "Good afternoon," she said, bowing slightly.

"Good afternoon." Marissa bowed as well. "I would like to leave a message for Takeshi Tanaka, please."

"Oh, I am so sorry." Aoi's expression became more business-like. "He is not here."

"I know." Marissa smiled and adjusted the tote on her

shoulder. "I just saw him in a black car driving by."

"Yes, he hired a private driver to take him to Osaka. His father was taken ill suddenly. He'd been visiting in Osaka, after the wedding."

Marissa felt despair, then astonishment. Takeshi had checked out of the ryokan! Her perfect ending had unfolded today, in almost a magical way. Now, the conclusion was not going to take place as she imagined. How could this be happening? If she hadn't been standing in a public place, she may have given way to tears.

Aoi seemed to sense Marissa's distress. "He asked for you before he left," she said. "I think he wanted to say goodbye to you."

Marissa felt her head nodding, slowly. "Yes. Yes, he waved at me. I saw the black sedan pass."

"Maybe, if you have his business card, you could send him an email."

Marissa attempted to keep her voice cheerful. "Thank you. I do have his card. I will take your suggestion." She managed to smile at the young woman in front of her. "In any case, I have my own packing to do." She bowed again before heading down the north hallway.

Thank goodness I don't have to fumble with a key. Marissa entered the genkan, kicked off her shoes and tossed her tote into a corner. After entering the bedroom, she sat on the floor, her back resting on the futon that had not been unrolled yet. She placed her head in her hands. *I should be happy. I did what I'd set out to do. Mission accomplished. Why do I feel so sad?*

Because life is moving on. I did what Brent asked me to do. That chapter in my life has closed, literally and figuratively. But in carrying out the mission, my own life continued. I met interesting people, some wise, some enigmatic. I encountered different value systems that challenged me. I've reaped so many benefits by spending a brief space of time in this culture. I even experimented with reinventing myself.

Marissa mentally laughed at her last thought. She'd always hated the word *reinvent*. She needed to reconsider her feelings about it. She had to admit, her experiences in Japan had brought new possibilities concerning its meaning to her awareness.

She retrieved her tote from the *genkan* and found the envelope containing her geisha pictures. She placed both of them on the countertop. The white matte makeup emphasized her eyes and lips, and the black wig wasn't as stark looking as she'd imagined. The kimono and hair ornament were both colorful and beautiful.

Hard to believe this image is me. Maybe this experience was a pivotal step in my journey forward as a person. I think I look impressive, even though it is very clear that I'm not Japanese and would never pass for an Asian. But the experience shows me that I have new possibilities ahead.. I've made few changes in the last year. Maybe it is my time to work on my self-development.

She'd love to know how Takeshi would have responded to the photographs. She would have watched him carefully for his first micro-expression, the clue to his first impression that he might be able to keep hidden except for that first nanosecond. She could consider scanning one of the photos and attaching it to an email. It wouldn't be the same as a conversation, though. But Takeshi needed to attend to his own family needs at this space, in this time.

Marissa heard a faint tapping noise. "Marissa-san?" The voice was feminine. *Mrs. Nakamura*! Marissa ran to the door, glad that she'd had a few moments to compose herself. She opened the door to the hallway. "Hello, Mrs. Nakamura." Seeing her new friend brought a smile to her face.

"Forgive me." Mrs. Nakamura lowered her eyes before meeting hers again. "I apologize for intruding. But I know you will leave soon, and I wondered…"

"If I found the temple?" Marissa finished the sentence for her when Mrs. Nakamura's voice trailed off. "Yes, I did find it. Thanks to Tom, the brother of your son-in-law. He gave me a suggestion, saying it could be a long shot. But he was correct. And the cherry blossoms at the Rokusonno shrine were not blown off in yesterday's winds."

"Ah. So it was Rokusonno! It is one of the smaller, less-well-known shrines."

"Yes, Tom suggested I could be looking for a shrine and not a temple. And something of the background of my photo suggested the right place." Marissa realized she'd been chattering at a rapid clip; she needed to stop and catch her breath. "I'm so grateful to you, Mrs. Nakamura. Without your help, I wouldn't have found the spot." Marissa grabbed the links of her necklace and held out the pendant. "I carried my husband's ring with me today, on this necklace. You can see it is gone now. It has found a new home, in the pond, among the koi and the stones. It belongs there."

"I can tell this story brings you peace." Mrs. Nakamura smiled broadly, and Marissa saw her teeth, maybe for the first time. Like her pearls, they were perfectly spaced. "I am hoping for a safe journey and that your life, when you get home, is full of blessings."

"Thank you. Thank you, Mrs. Nakamura." Marissa blinked back a tear. "You are one of the cherished friends I have met here. You'll always have a place in my heart. And if you ever come to Washington D.C., you can also have a place at my home while you are visiting. I don't think I gave you one of my business cards." Marissa went to her tote and fished out her card holder. She offered Mrs. Nakamura one, and was offered hers in return.

"Thank you, Marissa-san. Now, I have something to give you."

"Give me?"

Mrs. Nakamura produced a small velvet bag with a drawstring. She loosened the opening and extracted a string of pearls, similar to the ones she was wearing. "Before I met my husband, I was actively pursuing my career. I received a bonus at the end of my first year of employment due to my hard work on a special project. I also had a little gift money from my parents and used these funds to buy myself a pearl necklace. About a year after that, I met my future husband, who also gave me a necklace, the one I wear often." Her fingers went to the strand around her neck. "Both are Mikimoto. I would be honored for you to have these." She lifted the hand holding the velvet pouch and the pearls. "Maybe you could wear them to your friend's wedding?"

"Mrs. Nakamura! I don't know what to say."

Mrs. Nakamura smiled again as she returned the pearls to the bag and placed it in Marissa's hand. "Maybe arigato gozaimasu?"

Marissa felt tears swell her eyes. "Arigato gozaimasu. A thousand times. I'm overwhelmed."

"I wish you happiness, Marissa. I think you will find it."

To hell with Japanese etiquette! Marissa wrapped Mrs. Nakamura in a bear hug. The Japanese woman did not object.

"I must go now," Mrs. Nakamura said. "I will leave early in the morning for Tokyo. Safe travels."

"Safe travels." Marissa repeated as her friend bowed and walked away. She sighed as Mrs. Nakamura turned a corner and disappeared. She couldn't procrastinate any longer. She needed to pack to be ready for the morning. Her adventure in Japan was coming to an end. But hopefully, other adventures would await her at home. It was difficult for her to imagine that scenario, though.

I need to get home for Helen's wedding. And, of course, my students are counting on my return, too. But I wish I could try to find some way to extend my stay in this wonderful and enigmatic place.

CHAPTER TWENTY: LEAVING JAPAN, DAY SEVEN

The elderly Japanese woman in the aisle seat appeared to be napping. Grateful for her window seat on the Kyoto-to-Narita bus, Marissa turned her head toward the glass and let tears fall on her lap. She didn't feel sad, exactly. Overwhelmed, maybe. Her vague, lurking emotion needed to be released, whatever it was. Her life had been changed in ways she couldn't have predicted. *How will I cope with the ordinary again?*

She tried to focus on the immediate future. Helen's wedding wouldn't be ordinary. It would help to have her friend's big event in the first days of her resumption of daily life. But, once that ceremony was over…what then? She'd deal with it, one day at a time. Marissa tried to mentally rehearse her toast to the newlywed couple and imagined herself in the lavender dress. She really did like the gown and how well it fit her, and Mrs. Nakamura's pearls might be the perfect accent. She'd have to try them on with it. Maybe she could send a picture of herself in the gown to Takeshi, in addition to one of her geisha photos.

Marissa sat upright. The woman next to her opened her eyes wide at her abrupt movement. "It's okay," Marissa said aloud, even though she wasn't sure if the woman could understand her. She dug her cell phone out of her purse and skimmed through her contacts. Yes, she had the number for a hair stylist Helen had recommended. She needed to make an appointment for the morning of the wedding. As soon as she had internet available, she'd send a text to the salon.

It appeared that they were approaching the airport; people were reaching above and below their seats to collect belongings. Ten minutes later, the bus pulled into Narita's departure area. Marissa retrieved her rolling suitcase from the compartment under the bus and dragged it behind her into the terminal. She followed the crowd and got in line to go through Immigration. Once she was in the waiting area for her flight, she could relax. She located her passport and put it in the outside pocket of her tote.

She had to wait in line for about twenty minutes, but the process seemed relatively painless. Her passport was stamped and returned to her. She searched the overhead signs for the C concourse. There was a little convenience kiosk along the corridor. She stopped and used some of her remaining yen to buy a few *onigiri*, probably her last rice balls for a while. She stashed them in her tote, she'd nibble on the treats in a few minutes while waiting for boarding to start.

Marissa followed the signs to Concourse C, passing retail kiosks lining the passageway. She slowed when she noted the Mikimoto placard. A young Japanese woman with perfectly applied makeup stood behind the small counter.

Marissa thought of Brent's credit card. She hadn't spent any funds from it yet. Thanks to Mrs. Nakamura, she had a pearl necklace. Maybe she could buy a pair of quality pearl earrings. If the necklace complimented her lavender dress, she'd wear the earrings, too. She would always think of them as a gift from Brent.

Marissa stopped in front of the kiosk. "I'm looking for a pair of pearl earrings," she explained. "More than simple posts. But not too dangly."

"Of course." The young woman pulled out a tray from under the counter. "We have several pairs that you might like. Are you looking for white pearls, or something different?"

"White. Definitely white."

"Here is one pair." The young woman extracted a small box from the tray. She picked up an earring featuring two pearls; one anchoring the post and a larger one hanging from a short platinum chain. Marissa held it up to her ear. *Perfect!*

"I love these." Marissa said. "I'll take them." She handed the clerk the credit card she'd found in the envelope with Brent's message. "If there's not enough funds on this credit card, I have another one."

"Certainly." The clerk rang up the sale. "You have enough on this card. Here is your receipt. You will see your card's balance at the bottom." She placed the earring box in a black and white bag and handed it to Marissa with the receipt.

"Arigato gozaimasu." Marissa wondered if she'd verbalized her last thank you on Japanese soil. At least, on this trip.

She found a seat in her flight's waiting area and ate a rice ball while smoothing out the receipt from the Mikimoto kiosk with her free hand. Her earrings cost almost five hundred dollars, about what she'd expected. She glanced at the bottom of the slim slip of paper and resisted the urge to do a double take. Balance: $4510.00. *Brent had given her a $5000.00 credit card! How had he come up with that amount of money?*

A voice announced the flight to Washington D. C. in English. After waiting in a snaking line, she ambled down the jetway and the large plane's aisles until she reached her window seat toward the back. She dozed until the flight attendants began their departure announcements. A man stowed a briefcase under the seat next to hers, before sitting and fastening his seatbelt. The huge plane raced down the runway and became airborne.

The day had been slightly overcast, but once at altitude, the clouds dispersed, and Marissa could view the coast of Japan meeting the Pacific. *This is it, I'm really leaving*. Maybe in the next thirteen hours, she'd adjust to the idea of being back home in the Washington D. C. suburbs.

The man sitting next to her appeared to be American, probably a businessman, she thought. He looked vaguely familiar. It took a few minutes, but she realized the man was the tourist she'd run into at *Nijo* Castle and *Heian* Shrine. His beard was gone, but the reddish eyebrows and blue eyes were ones she'd seen before. And he wasn't wearing his signature red sneakers.

Marissa watched him take a briefcase out from under the seat in front of him. He pulled down his tray table before removing a file of papers from the briefcase. Red pen in hand, he directed his attention toward the sheet of paper on top. Marissa saw him jot a few words on it. "I didn't recognize you for a moment."

The man looked at her, right eyebrow raised. "Have we met?"

"Briefly." Marissa nodded. "Once at *Nijo* Castle, and

then again at *Heian* Shrine. I almost didn't recognize you without your red shoes."

"Oh, yes." The man's puzzled expression gave way to a smile. "I remember you now. Especially *Heian*. Those red shoes…the color definitely helped me find them quickly at the Japanese attractions where you left your footwear behind."

"I'll have to remember that advice for my next trip. Are you a teacher?" Marissa asked, gesturing toward the stack of papers.

He set his pen down. "Is it that obvious?"

"It is to another teacher."

"Yeah. Trying to catch up on my grading. I had good intentions of getting some of this done while I was in Tokyo, but too many distractions."

"Japan is beautiful," Marissa said. "And interesting. I don't blame you. There's time enough to grade on the way home. It's a long flight."

"Yes." He set his pen on the tabletop. "I'm Jeff Guzman. I teach psychology at Georgetown."

"Ah. I teach Comp Lit just outside the DC area, in Maryland."

Jeff nodded. "I was visiting a fellow professor in

Tokyo. He's involved in some sort of exchange program. I may try to enroll in the program in a year or two. I really enjoyed Tokyo and interacting with his students."

"That would be an opportunity." Marissa nodded. "Maybe I should investigate something like that. I was beginning to feel so comfortable in Japan."

"Do you have a business card with you?" Jeff asked. "I could send you the information I have stored on my campus computer."

"I do. I brought plenty of cards, since I heard the Japanese exchange them frequently."

"I did the same." Jeff peeked in the folding pocket of his briefcase. "Here's one of mine. Slightly dog-eared, I'm afraid."

"I can still read it." Marissa retrieved one of her cards from her tote. "Here you go."

A flight attendant rolled a cart next to Jeff's armrest and offered them tea and finger towels. "Lunch is coming soon," she said. She served them matcha and left the warm towels on their tray tables before rolling her cart down the aisle.

"That's one bonus on these overseas flights," Jeff said. "They feed you often, and well. To keep you occupied, I think."

Marissa laughed. "Well, I'm always up for a good meal."

"I am, too. And I'm getting hungry now. Didn't eat much on my mad dash to the airport."

"I just ate a rice ball. I'm addicted to those things. But, I'm sure I'll put away whatever they serve up."

"Is your husband in Japan?"

Marissa found herself speechless for a minute. She was still wearing her ring. Maybe she should move it to her right hand. "Well, I left part of him there," she said. Then she gasped. Her wording was terrible. It would look terribly inappropriate to laugh. "I'm sorry, but your question surprised me."

"No, I'm the one who should be sorry. I can sometimes be very blunt to the point of being rude. I apologize."

"Not at all. It's just that, well, I went to Japan to honor a wish of my husband's. You see, I'm a widow. My husband died just over a year ago."

"Oh, I'm so sorry. For your loss, of course. And for being so rude."

"No, don't worry about it. My husband wanted me to leave his ring in a specific place that we went to on our honeymoon. That was the reason for my trip."

"I see." Jeff closed his briefcase and returned it to the space under the seat.

The attendant came through again, with a larger cart. After collecting the finger towels, she refilled their teacups and served them a tray with beef, rice, fruit cup and a small salad. The sizzling beef smelled delicious. Marissa's stomach rumbled a little.

She and Jeff engaged in small talk about their respective schools until the lunch trays were collected. "Now it's going to get weird," Jeff said. "We're flying against the sun, so it will get dark soon. Then, we'll see the sun come up, probably as we hit the west coast, and we'll arrive in D. C. about the same time we left Japan."

"Yes, I noticed the departure and arrival times for this flight were almost identical," Marissa said. "And yes, that *is* weird. I wonder how the flight attendants keep track of the date and time. If they're on trans-Pacific flights, they must fly over the international date line often."

The cabin lights were dimmed. Jeff turned on his overhead light and resumed grading. Marissa reclined her seat and dozed off.

Carts were being wheeled down the aisle again. More finger towels. Another meal?

Jeff was reading a paperback. "I'm jealous. You were asleep for almost three hours. I can never sleep on a plane."

Marissa's eyebrows went up. "Three hours! I never can sleep on planes either. Usually." She wiped her hands on the warm towel. "I take it they're bringing us more food?"

"Looks like it. I think it is officially a snack this time. We'll get a breakfast about two hours before landing."

"I can handle a snack. Another meal would be a bit much."

The attendant brought them tea and a Danish with a side of fruit. Marissa ate and drank quickly before retrieving her pocket-sized notebook from her tote. She paged through it until she found her last draft of the wedding toast. She could do a little fine-tuning, maybe even memorize the speech. It would be ideal if she could deliver it spontaneously. Usually, she could handle this type of speaking without a problem, but she was afraid of two things; the effects of jet lag and the intrusion of powerful emotions. It would probably be best to keep the speech brief.

Her toast, in general, sounded reasonably dignified. Which is as it should be, she thought. Still, should she add a joke or two? Some inside information about her relationship with Helen through the years? They'd known each other more than half their lives, after all. They'd shared a lot of history. But much of that history involved Brent, at least indirectly. She'd have to think carefully about it. Of course, if she rehearsed her speech enough, it might become more rote to her, and less likely to result in an emotional meltdown.

"You look like you're practicing something," Jeff said.

"You're right, I am." Marissa smiled as she closed her notebook. "I have a good friend who is getting married within days of my return. I have the honor of toasting the couple at the reception. Helen and I have been friends for twenty years, so I want to be sure that I do a good job. And, in addition to everything else, I'm worried about jet lag."

"When is the wedding?"

Marissa laughed. "Well, I'm not sure what day it is at this place and time, but it's two days after I arrive home. Wait, that's the rehearsal. The wedding itself is three days from now. I think."

Jeff gave a small wave of his hand. "You'll be fine. Just give yourself time to reacclimate. And it looks like you've already prepared the speech. You're in good shape."

"I hope so."

After the snack trays were removed, Jeff started grading

in earnest. Marissa worked on the toast for a while, then put the notebook away. She may need to make a few last-minute changes, but she was satisfied with what she'd written and felt like Helen would like it, too. She perused the movies available on the small screen in front of her and chose a lighthearted comedy. The film would distract her until they were closer to D. C.

She must have dozed off again. Jeff's snoring woke her. She'd tease him about that when he woke up. She allowed herself to think about Takeshi. She had his business card safely packed away. She could email him. But how would he view that action? Would his Japanese upbringing recognize her email as improper? Or would his American education lead him to accept it, maybe even welcome it?

Of course, Takeshi had her email address as well. The likelihood of seeing him again was probably slim. But the exchange program Jeff was talking about could be a possibility. Marissa could get used to the idea of living in Japan for an extended period. She'd investigate the program, once the wedding was over.

A serving cart started to rumble down the aisle again and Jeff woke up. "I guess I did fall asleep, after all."

"Probably those student papers. I've found some of my own grading to be the cure for insomnia."

Trays featuring an American breakfast and coffee were

set before them. Marissa eagerly sipped the strong brew, she needed something to boost her alertness to help her get through customs and find a ride home. The next time she fell asleep, it would be in her own bed. In spite of her longing to stay in Japan, the idea of sleeping in her own bed was very appealing.

The flight attendant collected the trays and brought a customs form. There was an item asking about plants and seeds. She did have the little packet that the schoolgirl gave her at the Golden Temple. Surely, that would be okay to bring into the country. It was a type of souvenir item, really. She checked "no". The colorful packet was tucked in an interior pocket of her purse. She wouldn't mention it.

Marissa wondered how close they were to the east coast, they'd been over land for quite a while. She'd noted a large river just after the breakfast trays were collected. She wondered if it could be the Ohio, or maybe a stream on its way to the Atlantic. They must be getting close to Washington.

The announcement came after the breakfast cart retreated down the aisle. "Ladies and gentlemen, we will be landing in about fifteen minutes. Please stow all of your belongings and return your seats to their upright position. Keep your customs form where it can be easily retrieved."

Jeff stretched. "Well, I have to say, the time went fairly

quickly. Fortunately, I have a day off tomorrow before I return to the university. How about you?"

"I have to go to campus for a few hours tomorrow to get organized, but no classes yet. I'll sleep well before then, I'm sure. It won't be too stressful."

Their landing was smooth, and they approached the gate. Once deplaning was allowed, Jeff jumped up with his briefcase. "Nice to meet you, Marissa. I'll email you soon." He made it about ten feet down the aisle before other passengers stepped in his way.

Marissa moved into his vacated seat and retrieved her belongings. Since she was seated in the rear of the plane, she knew she'd be one of the last to leave. She followed the trail of other passengers to customs and waited in line. Finally, she was summoned to an officer. After the usual questions, he asked her about the agricultural products she was bringing back.

"None." Marissa said. "I was in urban areas for the entire trip." The official looked at a page of her passport and stamped it, before waving her through. Marissa picked up her tote and purse and strode into a large hallway. An image of the tiny girl who'd interviewed her near the Golden Temple rose in her memory. She could see her bright brown eyes and glossy bangs. She needed to hold on to that seed packet.

Her suitcase careened near the edge of the baggage

carousel on the airport's lower level. Marissa called for an Uber. Forty minutes later, she unlocked her front door.

Her eyes darted around the surroundings, everything seemed familiar. Everything, that is, except the face that looked back at her from the foyer's decorative mirror.

CHAPTER TWENTY-ONE: HELEN'S WEDDING

Marissa had to hand it to Helen, her strategy concerning the bridesmaid's regalia was a huge success. Helen had provided her attendants with guidelines regarding length and color of their gowns but had allowed them to choose their own. Marissa scanned the line of women who stood across the front of the church. All wore various shades of pink and lavender and all looked lovely. Sandy's athletic physique and Helen's cousin's five-foot-one-inch frame were each flattered by the gowns they'd chosen. Helen had made no stipulations concerning Marissa's attire, but the lavender full-length gown she'd chosen fit right in. Mrs. Nakamura's pearls added a stunning touch, as did her new earrings.

Helen herself looked amazing. Her dress with its simple train, the natural flower headdress holding her cascading veil, the stephanotis and ivy bouquet...all of it came together perfectly. Once Marissa saw her best friend at the rehearsal, she let go of all the grudges she'd held during their trans-Pacific communication.

Helen, as a mature woman planning her first wedding, had done a phenomenal job. She'd done it singlehandedly, because her mother was in a nursing home and in no position to help plan anything. Even her mother's attendance required some orchestrating, but she sat in the first pew on the bride's side.

Marissa focused on the music, the readings, and the vows. The ceremony was brief, and the recessional started before she had a chance to even think about getting weepy. Marissa took a deep breath as the newlyweds marched down the aisle. She'd made it through the wedding of her best friend without any kind of melt-down. Even though the toast, her contribution to the event, was still to come, Marissa felt herself relax. She could handle the toast without any problem, now that the ceremony was over and her eyes were still dry.

Marissa exited the pew with the others in her row and waited in the hall underneath the sanctuary with the wedding party. There would be pictures in the church after the guests departed for the reception. In theory, Marissa was free to leave, too, but due to the transportation arrangements of the day, she was not. Helen had sent a limo to pick her up that morning, along with the bridesmaids. "You've only been back a couple of days. I don't want to even think of you falling asleep behind the wheel on your way home from the reception."

Marissa hadn't complained too much. There were advantages to having a guaranteed ride. She could be free of any worry regarding the combination of jet lag and alcohol at the reception.

The photographer directed the wedding party back upstairs and Marissa took a seat in one of the back pews. This time, she sat on the groom's side and got her first chance to scrutinize the groomsmen when they were completely oblivious to her. She'd been introduced to them the previous evening at the rehearsal dinner, but they'd been seated at another table and she'd had little interaction with them.

She knew the best man was Aaron, Chad's older brother. The others were Ted, Zach, and Todd. She guessed they ranged in age from 35 to 45. All were athletic-looking and only Todd wore a ring on his left hand. Instinctively, Marissa's hand went to her neck, searching for the infinity symbol pendant. A moment of panic ensued before she remembered placing it in her jewelry case the previous evening. Mrs. Nakamura's pearls were around her neck now.

She watched as the photographer paired each of the groomsmen with a bridesmaid. Next, all attendants were called to the front for several group shots of the entire wedding party. A few shots with just the matron of honor, best man and the bridal couple came next. The photographer announced he was done with the attendants and gave them permission to leave.

Sandy came down the aisle toward Marissa. "Hey, you!" she said, wrapping an arm around Marissa's waist and giving her a quick hug. "Let's find our limo and get to the reception. These shoes are killing me. As soon as the dance floor opens, I'm ditching these things." She lifted her skirt to reveal a pair of hot pink pumps. "I came prepared. I brought a pair of ballet slippers along in my purse."

Marissa joined her in the church aisle. "You're always the practical and smart one. I wish I'd thought of ballet slippers. I'm sure my feet will be screaming by the time the reception winds down. By the way, you look fantastic. Great dress, the style and color are so flattering! Where'd you get it?"

"You'll never believe this." Sandy lowered her voice as if she was sharing a government secret. "My mom knows a dressmaker. I just went to her and told her what I wanted, in general terms. She made a sketch, told me how much yardage I'd need, and I came back after buying the fabric I wanted. And voila!" Sandy twirled around in the aisle. "I was afraid that anything off the rack would be too frou-frou."

"Wow. I'll have to get the name of your dressmaker. I'm sure the one I used at my wedding has retired. Was it expensive?"

"Not really. I bet I paid less than any of the other bridesmaids. But hey, you don't look too shabby yourself!"

"Thanks." Marissa glanced down at her gown. "I just happened to find this when I wasn't even looking. I really do like it. I think it helps when you feel comfortable with what you're wearing. And I definitely feel comfortable in this."

"Well, you look great. The color is perfect for you. Come on, let's find the limo and get out of here. Hopefully the bar will be open when we arrive!"

Two limousines waited at the curb. Evidently, all the other attendants were inside. The drivers insisted that Sandy and Marissa split up for the ride to the reception hall. Marissa felt a little disappointed, she looked forward to sharing some of the details of her trip to Kyoto with Sandy. Instead, she was practically sitting on Zach's lap, which was more than a little awkward. Still, the reception was less than two miles away.

"Sorry, Zach. I hope I'm not crowding you."

"Not a problem," he said, flashing brilliantly white teeth. "At least you're not wearing a puffy skirt. You look fantastic, by the way."

"Oh! Ah, thanks." Marissa was unprepared for the compliment. *Zach must've had his teeth chemically whitened for this event. And should I compliment his appearance? He does look good, but I'm assuming he's wearing rented formalwear.*

The limo rounded a sharp corner. A couple of bridesmaids shrieked, then laughed, sparing Marissa from having to reply. "We're almost there," Zach said. "I was at a reception at this hall a couple of years ago. It's a pretty cool place. Nice dance floor."

"Oh, good. I've been to so many receptions where the dance floor was tiny." *That was a dumb comment. Makes it sound like you want to dance with this guy. But, maybe that wouldn't be so bad.*

The limo stopped. The driver sprang to the curb and opened Marissa's door. He had to grab her elbow to keep her from falling out. "Sorry," he said. "I guess you guys were really packed in there."

Marissa laughed. "It's okay. We were crammed in the back seat, that's for sure. But the ride was short." Zach extricated himself from the limo, and Helen's petite cousin appeared next.

Zach made a move toward Marissa and she wondered if he intended to take her arm. "Excuse me a minute, will you?" Marissa said. "My contribution to this event is coming up. I'm toasting the couple, so I'm going to isolate myself for a few minutes and go over the speech. I'm sure I'll see you later."

"You've got that right." Zach flashed another smile at her that looked like a toothpaste ad. "I hope you brought your dancing shoes."

Marissa tried to smile. She looked at the second limo, hoping that Sandy would come to her rescue. She wasn't disappointed.

"Sandy, do you know if there's a private area inside where I could go over my toast a couple of times? I just would like to relax and get my head together for 5 to 10 minutes. Some peace and quiet is what I need right now."

"I'm sure there's someplace. Let's go in and ask."

They walked under the striped canopy and Sandy approached a young woman standing in the reception area. She had maroon hair and wore dark red, almost black, lipstick which didn't compliment her pale skin. Her skirt was black and very short, displaying black fishnet stockings. Marissa was struck by the contrast to Aoi. *Nothing like a little goth detail at a wedding.*

"Excuse me," Sandy said. "My friend was wondering if there's a private area where she could rehearse the toast to the bride and groom."

"Sure." The receptionist answered. "We have a bride's room. Sometimes we have the ceremonies at our facility, too. The bride's room isn't needed today, so you're welcome to use it. Just follow me." She opened a door that led to a stairwell. Marissa followed her downstairs to a small room lined with mirrors and featuring several tissue boxes.

"Thanks. I'll only need this space for a few minutes."

"That's fine. Just turn the lights out when you leave." The receptionist left, and Marissa sat on a stool in front of a counter that probably was meant as a makeup application area. The room lacked windows, and the only light was fluorescent. Marissa looked at herself in the mirror. *I look ghastly. So pale.* She hoped the tone of her complexion was a result of the artificial lighting. *Why didn't I bring makeup with me? I could use a touch-up. At least I have a lipstick. If I can, I should reapply it right before the toast. I'm sure there will be a photo or two.*

Marissa swiveled the stool so she wouldn't have to face her own reflection. She opened her purse and removed the small notebook where she'd written the final draft of her speech. She didn't think she'd need to refer to it, but she'd brought it, just in case. She recited the words, made a few corrections, then repeated the full speech again. *Done.* She could handle this. She grabbed a handful of tissues and added them to her purse, just in case. She refreshed her lipstick before she stood. Her complexion did look better when she wasn't under the direct glare of the lights.

A flurry of billowing white came through the hall's front door as Marissa reached the top of the stairwell. Helen and Chad had arrived. Guests clapped and cheered. Sandy caught Marissa's eye. "C'mon. I think they want to have the dinner started quickly, so we can get on to the partying."

Marissa followed Sandy to the table prepared for the bridal party. She found her name card at the end of the long banquet table situated along a huge window overlooking the green gardens of the establishment. The guests would have a panoramic view of the outdoors, but the bridal party faced inward. Marissa noted that she'd be sitting next to Zach. He would be her only dinner conversation partner most likely, with her place at the end and no one seated on the opposite side of the table.

Helen and Chad took their positions at the banquet table's center and the rest of the bridal party found their seats. "Hey, I guess we're stuck with each other, again." Zach grinned as he stood behind his chair.

"I hope I won't bore you," Marissa said. She made an effort to return his smile. Where was she at this point in space and time? She was at her best friend's wedding and she should participate in the spirit of the festivities. "I'm a little nervous about the toast. Hopefully, it will go okay."

"You got the chance for your little practice session,

right? It should go fine." Zach waved his hand as if to dismiss her worries.

Helen clinked on her glass until the background conversation in the room decreased in volume. "The wait staff will be serving dinner soon. So, please find your seats. If you have a drink in hand take it with you. They'll be pouring champagne toward the end of the meal, for the toast."

Marissa felt a few tiny butterflies flitting around in her stomach at the mention of the toast. Helen had told her she wanted it at the end of the meal, before the cake cutting and the dance floor officially opening. *I need to eat something. Hopefully the food will be tempting.*

The minister who had officiated at the church ceremony offered grace. The servers came out immediately with trays bearing meals for the bridal party. Salad and bread were already on the table.

At least we're being served first. I don't need to wolf down my food. Marissa picked up her knife and fork. She sampled the chicken and the beef on her plate. Each was garnished with a sauce and both were delicious. The vegetables were also tasty; cooked enough, but not mushy.

"Hey, this is actually good." The comment came from Zach. "Last time I was here as a guest, the food was just so-so."

"I agree with you." Marissa helped herself to a roll from the breadbasket. "Being served first probably doesn't hurt, either."

"Yeah. Everything's hot, but not reheated." Evidently Zach really liked the steak. He'd polished off most of it. "So, tell me a little bit about you. How long have you known Helen?"

"Most of my adult life. We went to grad school at the same university. Became roommates our second year there, and best friends ever since. Helen and I have been through a lot together. She's stood by me through several events, even more than family did."

"Sounds like the water between you is thicker than blood."

Marissa laughed. "Interesting way to put it. I guess you could say that."

Marissa could see the DJ setting up his equipment at the back of the ballroom area. After plugging in several cords, he picked up a microphone. He tapped on it gently before saying "May I have your attention!" He walked toward the bridal table. "Ladies and gentlemen, it's time for one of the sometimes sentimental, sometimes humorous and always traditional events of the wedding celebration. The toasts to the bride and groom. I'd like to announce Marissa Shively, friend of the bride."

So soon! Marissa had imagined having a minute to prepare. Well, she was prepared. She found her small notebook, opened to the correct page, and grabbed a few tissues.

"Don't forget your champagne flute." Zach handed it to her.

"Oh, thanks!" *That would be awkward, not having a glass to toast with!* Marissa walked to the center of the platform. There was a small space between the long tables for the attendants and the central table for the bride and groom. She stood in the space, and laid her tiny notebook, tissues and champagne flute on the corner of the bridal table. Servers began pouring champagne.

The DJ came forward and handed her a cordless mic. Holding a mic, another thing she hadn't considered, or planned for. She held it in her left hand and opened her notebook to the page where she'd jotted her speech. She glanced at the first sentence. She could do this.

Marissa turned to face Helen and Chad. Seeing her friend looking so beautiful and happy took her breath away. Helen was her friend. She deserved the happiness she exuded today. Marissa forced herself to inhale. Suddenly, she was overwhelmed with emotion. She made it through the ceremony, how could she be on the verge of tears now?

Sandy leaned forward from behind Chad's shoulder. She smiled and gave Marissa a "thumbs up" sign. Marissa took a second deep breath, and this one echoed around the room, thanks to the microphone. Where was she in space and time? She was at her best friend's wedding. Her job was to contribute to the celebration. And that is what she would do.

Marissa looked straight at her friend, ignoring the open notebook. Then, she surveyed the guests sitting at the circular tables in front of her. *Whoa. There's a lot of them.*

"Helen and Chad, members of the bridal party, and honored guests: I've just come back from a trip out of town. While I was gone, I worked on the speech for this special day. I thought I had it just about perfect. But now, I realize I need to put it aside and say what is in my heart at this moment."

She turned to face her friend. "Helen, you look amazing. You've always been a beautiful person, inside and out, so that's no surprise. It's obvious how extraordinarily happy you are today. And you deserve to be.

"Chad, you are one lucky man. Because I've known Helen for almost twenty years, I can attest to her faithfulness and her unselfishness. She will be your companion through the best of times and the worst. She won't desert you when the chips are down. I know this, because she's never deserted me, her friend, when I've been at the best times and the worst points of my life. She's been truly happy for my successes and commiserated with me during the sad times. We'd all like to think friends like this are common, but the truth is – we know they are rare.

"So be assured, you have found the perfect life companion in Helen. The sparks I see flying between the two of you today will be there for a lifetime. I offer you both my most sincere congratulations." Marissa held up the champagne glass that had been filled by the attentive server. "Here's to Helen and Chad."

Guests and attendants raised their glasses. A few said, "To the bride and groom!" or "Congratulations!"

After a minute, the DJ/emcee stepped forward and took the mic. He announced the best man and handed the microphone to Aaron. Marissa moved toward her seat. She heard Aaron say something about being a hard act to follow and an undercurrent of polite laughter from the attendees.

"Damn, that was good." Zach stood and pulled out her chair.

Marissa shrugged. "You know, I worked and worked on that toast, especially on the flight home. I thought I'd finally reached the perfect speech. But, today, I knew it wasn't right."

"No worries. You did give the perfect toast. I feel kind of sorry for Aaron."

The guests erupted in laughter at something Aaron had just said.

"Nah. The crowd needs some comic relief right now. His speech is a good contrast."

Marissa lent out a pent-up breath and drained her champagne glass. She hadn't admitted to herself how heavily the responsibility of the toast had weighed on her. Now, she could truly relax. Aaron ended his speech and there was another toast. Marissa pretended to drink from her now-empty flute, hoping no one had seen her down its entire contents earlier.

The DJ announced that the cake would be cut in about ten minutes. Following that ceremony, the dance floor would be open.

"You strike me as a serious person, Marissa," Zach said.

"That's a pretty fair assessment, I guess," Marissa responded. "I mean, I went to graduate school and I teach college students. I like discovering new ideas. Does that make me a serious person?"

"I think so," Zach said. "But maybe, today, you can discover how to have a good time. Listen, I have to do this official first dance thing with a bridesmaid at the other end of the table. But I'm reserving the second dance for you, okay?"

Marissa nodded. "Sure."

CHAPTER TWENTY-TWO: ONE YEAR LATER

Sunlight peeked between the slats of Marissa's bedroom shades. *So nice to have a little extra time to sleep on Friday mornings!* The days were getting longer, the sun was above the horizon and a few songbirds seemed to be holding a competition for the most melodious morning song. Marissa pulled on a pair of jeans and her jacket before retrieving the newspaper from her driveway, but only after starting the coffee in her four-cup coffee maker. She'd need to head to campus in a little bit, but her Friday schedule allowed her the luxury of an hour to lounge around and read the headlines. The routine had become a welcome stress-relieving ritual at the end of the work week.

Marissa poured herself a cup of coffee and unfolded the newspaper to reveal the front page of its Weekend section: a panoramic view of the Tidal Basin cherry blossoms. The photo had to be from their archives. Most of this year's cherry blossoms had not bloomed yet, at least that was the word on the previous evening's eleven o'clock news. But the weather experts agreed they'd bloom over the next few days. Marissa was tempted to go down to the basin on Saturday. An early start via the Metro would be required to beat the crowds and eliminate the frustration of hunting for a parking spot.

Her gaze wandered over the kitchen and settled on the calendar pinned to the bulletin board near the refrigerator. Just one year ago, she'd been in the final stages of preparation for her trip to Japan. She'd hung the dress for Helen's wedding safely in the back of her closet and made sure everything was in order at the university. After frantically grading all outstanding papers and handing them back to students, she'd thrown clothes into a suitcase; checked and double-checked that Brent's ring was in a zippered pocket of her carry-on. The night before her departure, she'd awakened in a panic, dreaming that she'd left the ring at home.

She hadn't counted on forming friendships in Japan or having so many adventures in the space of a week. There was the stress of finding the shrine, and the relief of leaving the ring in the place Brent had chosen. Funny, she really hadn't thought much about Brent's ring since. Which was probably as it should be.

She dated a couple of men since returning to the Washington D. C. area. Zach was nice enough, but the only thing they had in common was their participation in Helen's wedding. Marissa thought Zach's main objective was finding someone to help him watch his daughter Zoe when he had custody of her, every other weekend. Zoe was a sweet child, but hardly the reason to form a relationship. She'd also gone out with Jeff, the Georgetown professor she'd met on the flight home. Their relationship never progressed beyond a platonic one. Their time together consisted of talking about their experiences in Japan, and his detailed information about the faculty exchange program. One bright spot in their friendship was his interest in her geisha pictures. He was truly an appreciative audience, a reaction that boosted Marissa's confidence. Jeff was spending a lot of time on his academic career in preparation for tenure. Marissa wondered if he was putting personal relationships on hold until his dossier was complete.

Marissa made her own inquiries about the exchange program and even downloaded an application. The people at the program's headquarters told her they were more interested in science and math instructors, but they considered all applications they received. She had hers almost finished and would mail it within a few days. She wondered what kind of chance she really had. Spending a year in Japan, and getting paid for it, sounded like a dream come true. *Nothing ventured, nothing gained.* She'd mail in her application and try to forget about it for a while.

Her thoughts turned to Takeshi. She'd emailed him a

New Year greeting and attached the best image from her self-indulgent geisha photo shoot. He'd responded with a New Year greeting of his own, but there'd been no communication since. Marissa also wondered about Yo, was he still cancer free? And Mrs. Nakamura! Marissa treasured the pearls she'd given her, and the history behind them. Maybe she'd write a short story about the Japanese widow's gift over the summer. The end of the spring semester was only a few weeks away. She'd have time for some creative pursuits during the summer months.

Marissa polished off her coffee. She stood to return to the coffee maker and pour a second cup when she experienced a sudden craving for tea. .*Ocha*, green tea. She wondered if she had loose tea leaves of any quality lurking in her cupboard. If she did, it would be the last dry leaves in a bag that once held a half-pound or more. After dragging her kitchen stool over to the cabinets that stored her more exotic teas, coffees, and spices, she stood on the stool's seat to look at the top shelf where she found a few almost-empty brown paper bags closed with twist ties. She decided to bring them down to the table. She'd inspect them all to decide if any held tea leaves worth brewing.

The doorbell rang before she had a chance to negotiate the stool's last step. She almost fell. Heart racing due to the close call, she rushed across the living room and threw open the front door. A red-and-yellow van was parked in her driveway, and the uniformed driver stood on her porch. "Marissa Shively?" he asked.

"That's me." Marissa was intrigued. Who could be sending her a package? She hadn't ordered anything.

She signed the clipboard the delivery man held for her. He handed her a carton, about the size of a small shoe box. It wasn't too heavy, but she could tell one side held most of its weight. She brought the package into her living room and set it on the coffee table. There were Japanese characters on the box. The shipping label was printed in English, though. Very neat block letters. The sender line read *Tanaka*.

The combination of coffee, the doorbell, and a package from Takeshi made her heart leap against the inside of her ribcage. She returned to the kitchen and came back with a pair of scissors. After slicing through the tape, she opened the box lid. The heavier part of the box held a delicate teapot with two matching cups without handles. All were painted with dainty pink cherry blossoms against a dove gray background. The lighter part of the box held a bag of tea. There was also an envelope with a bulge in the middle. Marissa's trembling fingers tore the envelope flap open and withdrew a single sheet along with a smaller envelope about the size of a luggage tag. The top and the bottom of the paper held Japanese characters. A message in English was centered on the paper.

Please enjoy the Gyokuro tea we shared in Kyoto's Gion district. Also, I think it is time to renew your good luck.

Takeshi Tanaka.

Marissa brought the box with its contents to the kitchen table, filled her teakettle with water and set it on the burner. *Definitely worthwhile to get a kettle going now.* While waiting for the water to boil, she washed the new teapot and cups. The pot had its own infuser inside. Marissa took her coffee measure and scooped tea into it. After the water came to a boil, she took the kettle off the flame and waited a full minute before pouring the water into the pot. Marissa paused and inhaled deeply before putting the lid over the steaming water. The unique aroma of the steeping tea leaves brought back memories of the evening she and Takeshi sat in the Gion district tea house. How they'd had a conversation and laughed together for the first time. He walked to the train station with her, and he told her the moon looked especially beautiful that evening.

Marissa opened the small packet. A white brocade amulet, resembling the one Takeshi had given her a year ago, tumbled onto the tabletop. Yes, Takeshi had warned her that the luck promoted by the original amulet would last only for one year. Now, she had an extension!

She paced back and forth, waiting for the tea to develop

its special flavor. She poured herself a cup and brought it back out to her coffee table. She could see spring blossoms visible in her neighbor's yards, but none of them were cherry. Maybe she could see about getting a cherry tree from a nursery. She still had the money from Brent's credit card gift. Maybe a cherry tree or two would be a fitting use for part of the money. She could drive around and visit a few nurseries on Sunday afternoon. Before any landscaping decisions, though, she needed to decide about selling the house.

The teacup felt warm, but not too hot, in her hand. She took a sip of the brewed tea. The flavor was subtle, yet the brew had a complex sweetness. *Must be the nature of the rare and pampered tea leaves that results in the unique taste.* Takeshi had said she was wise that night, almost a year ago. What would he say about this past year of hers? Was she spending her time wisely?

It had become her habit to go out for an early dinner with several of her colleagues after the Friday faculty meetings, and usually they'd take in a film as well. The group was mixed, both men and women, married and single. Sometimes spouses came along. They enjoyed each other's company, and Marissa had found the group to be the high point of her social life in recent months. *I don't know if that's a good thing, or a bad thing.* She shrugged, even though there was no one to see her gesture. *I guess it's been a good thing for me at this point in my life.*

She looked at the clock. *Almost time to head to campus.* She poured herself another cup of tea and took sips as she gathered her papers and files and put them in her briefcase. She ducked into the first-floor bathroom near the kitchen and put on a little make-up. She was glad to have a routine meeting to divert her attention for a little bit. But the thought of heading to the Tidal Basin the next morning had transitioned from an idea to a definite plan. Images from her time in Japan and plans for the following day competed for the space in her imagination.

I just hope I can concentrate on the meeting.

***

A whining alarm woke Marissa from a sound sleep. After stopping the annoying racket, she laid back and stretched on the pillows, grateful that she'd slept soundly. After the excitement of Takeshi's gifts, she'd wondered if sleep would be impossible. She jumped out of bed and showered before putting on her newest pair of jeans, a pink tee shirt that had been her favorite for the last year, and her white sneakers. A pink flowered scarf from her closet completed her ensemble. She felt tempted to wear Mrs. Nakamura's pearls, but decided she'd save them for something dressier than jeans.

She left home just before eight and was relieved to find the Metro wasn't crowded. Most passengers were engrossed in their cell phones, giving Marissa mental space to explore her own thoughts. Yo came to mind. Hopefully, his medical tests from the last year confirmed his cancer was nonexistent. She wished she had some way to contact him or his family. The origami crane he'd given her stood atop her dresser. And the little girl who'd interviewed her that first day, with her packet of seeds! Marissa had to laugh at her strategy of hiding the packet and sneaking it through customs. The memory of that little girl was now a part of her. She couldn't part with the seeds. Once home, she tucked them away safely with her other souvenirs. She needed to do a little online research before deciding to plant them.

The train was pulling into the Smithsonian Museum stop. She'd have a little hike to reach the Tidal Basin; but she'd prepared for the trek by wearing her athletic shoes. She slung her purse over her shoulder and walked up the stairs to street level.

It was humid close to the Potomac, but the temperature was pleasantly cool. She approached the Tidal Basin and saw the Jefferson Monument reflected in the still water. Small crowds of people clustered about. By eleven o'clock, she imagined the area would be mobbed.

She decided to walk around the basin to the Jefferson Monument, then take a leisurely stroll back. Maybe she'd find a spot where she could sit for a little while and quiet her mind in order to reflect on the past year. Maybe she'd even get some inspiration for the future. The idea of the pearl necklace story wasn't a bad one. She also needed to make a decision about her social life, too. Should she try online dating? Occasionally she'd get emails advertising "Meet Asian Women." Were there comparable services for women wanting to meet Asian men? She laughed out loud at the thought. She was only interested in one Asian man.

The cherry tree buds were swelling, and a quarter of them had bloomed. If the forecast for Saturday's weather was accurate, the sunshine could result in most of them opening by afternoon. The gentle drifting of falling blossoms could start any time.

About halfway to the Monument, she noticed a flat grassy area between two cherry trees. Maybe she'd sit there in a few minutes on her return trip.

After reaching the Jefferson Monument, she stood at the edge of the tidal basin and surveyed the panorama in front of her. The trees would look pinker tomorrow, but there were enough of the rosy blossoms on display to make for an astonishing vista. The ripple-free pool mirrored the trees' grandeur.

She stood for several minutes before turning away from the pool and retracing her steps along the path. *My spot between the trees is still unoccupied.* She headed for the patch of velvety grass between the two slightly twisted trunks and sat. A little dew remained on the grass, so reclining seemed risky. A stream of people paraded by her, focusing on the trees, the water, and the sky. The number of passers-by was increasing, but the noise level stayed low. She observed old and young faces with expressions ranging from peaceful to awestruck. There was little conversation among them. Marissa experienced a feeling of calm, yet connectedness. She felt immersed in the diverse stream of humanity. Was this the mental state the Japanese people experienced every year? Is this why the cherry blossoms were so esteemed? Last year, her search and the anxiety connected with it would not allow a sense of such serenity. She'd moved to a new time and place.

She heard a shuffle behind her. Probably someone approaching, perhaps led by a dog straining at its leash. She prepared herself to be prodded by a cold nose, perhaps licked by a Yorkie or poodle dragging its owner along toward the water.

Instead, two polished leather shoes came to rest near her left knee. Camel-colored trousers with a neatly pressed pleat rose above them.

"May I join you?" The voice was familiar. Masculine, refined.

Marissa twisted to her left and looked upward. Due to the angle of the sun, she couldn't see the man's features distinctly. The smooth voice resonated with a place in her memory.

"Takeshi!" The words sounded strange coming from her mouth. Marissa realized she'd rarely used his name aloud before this moment. She struggled to get to her feet, wishing she could do it in one smooth motion, but not really caring. She briefly felt his hand cup her elbow. Once she was face-to-face with him, she could see his features and a subtle smile. He looked the same as when they'd passed on the street, almost a year ago. The goodbye that she didn't recognize as a goodbye until it was too late.

"How did you find me?"

"I think I had good luck. But I planned to be persistent. I had a feeling you would come to the site of the cherry blossoms sometime this weekend. I was fortunate to find you so soon. I was prepared to wait."

A single cherry blossom floated by them. One of the first ones to fall, Marissa thought. She studied Takeshi's face more closely. Perhaps a suggestion of worry lurked behind his eyes, or maybe she saw jet lag and fatigue. "How is your father?"

Takeshi gave a little nod of his head. "He is well, thank you. But he was ill through most of last summer. His constitution is strong, though. He has returned to his business." He gestured with his right arm, and Marissa noticed the briefcase. "No files in this today." Takeshi popped it open. A neatly folded blanket took up most of the space inside. "You have found a good spot. Let us officially claim it." He spread the blanket on the ground, gesturing with his palm. "Have a seat. I will find a coffee vendor. It will not be as good as Tanaka coffee, but it should be fairly fresh this early in the day."

Marissa sat on the blanket. She watched Takeshi retreat from the Tidal Basin toward the bustle of the street. He was dressed more casually than she'd seen him in Japan, but still his appearance was neat. She guessed even his casual clothes were professionally tailored.

He'd probably find coffee nearby, but Marissa took advantage of the privacy and dug her cell phone out of her purse. She was supposed to meet up with Helen and Chad in mid-afternoon. Helen had dropped some broad hints that she might be bringing someone along. The situation might evolve into something of a blind date.

She typed in a text. "Can't make it today. I think a life changing event is happening." She double checked the recipient. *Eek! I almost texted my gynecologist's office!* She copied the message and sent it to Helen. Marissa looked over her shoulder. Takeshi may be returning, but if so, he was still too far away to be clearly identifiable.

She heard a ping from her phone. Helen was channeling the gynecology theme. "You're too young for menopause. Could you be pregnant?"

Marissa stifled the impulse to laugh out loud. She typed a quick reply. "None of the above. Details later. But not today." She turned her phone to Mute and put it back in her purse. She relaxed onto her elbows and stared up at the blossoms. The two trees above her displayed a mixture of buds, open flowers, and a few petals that were falling, or carried on the breeze.

She heard the rustle of footsteps on grass. Takeshi handed her a cardboard tray bearing two cups of coffee, cream and sugar, and a couple of stirrers. He sat beside her.

He took a sip from his Styrofoam cup. "Not too bad. The vendor had just finished brewing this."

Marissa sampled a little. "You're right. Actually, this is pretty good."

"Thank you for asking about my father. I apologize if this is too private, but how are you?"

"I'm doing well, thank you. In some ways, the last year has been a little strange. I can honestly say it has been a learning experience, though."

"Yes." Takeshi nodded and looked toward the basin. He sipped more coffee. He didn't speak for a while. Bird calls, background traffic sounds, and occasional words from passing sightseers filled the space.

Marissa felt comfortable with Takeshi's silence, his

expression indicated calm. "After seeing the cherry blossoms here this year, I think I understand what they mean to the people of Japan. At least, a little better than I did last year."

Takeshi nodded his head. "Yes. In Japan, you were under pressure to find a certain location. Now you are in a different place in your life."

"I am. A place where I can appreciate some things on a different level. After the stress of the last couple of years, I appreciate many aspects of everyday life more, to say nothing of the special events."

"Yes," Takeshi said. "When my father was ill, life became different. Tense. Now that he is well, I can relax and enjoy the world around me again."

Marissa noticed the crowds were increasing and getting noisier. Perhaps the more reverent observers arrived earlier in the morning.

"How long are you here?" she asked.

"Five more days. This area is my temporary base, I will make a few calls up and down the coast. Then on to Chicago, California and back to Japan."

"Maybe next year I'll return to Japan. I've applied for a teaching program. If I'm accepted, I could be teaching in Japan a year from September."

"Why not come back this summer?"

This summer! Why don't I? An image of the credit card that Brent had given her popped to the front of Marissa's brain. It was still in the bottom drawer of her jewelry box. She was not teaching summer school.

"I guess I could." Marissa paused. Where was she in this place and time? "I will."

Takeshi raised one eyebrow. "You will." His expression was quizzical, but his remark was a statement, not a question. He paused and took a sip of coffee.

Marissa turned to face him. "I think the sky is especially blue today."

Takeshi set his coffee cup back in the holder and turned to look into her eyes. "I agree with you, Marissa-san. And the sun is very bright."

GLOSSARY OF JAPANESE WORDS AND PHRASES

Arigato: "Thank you".

Bento: A Japanese style boxed lunch.

Chotto matte: "Wait a minute."

Genkan: Entry area to an interior space. There is a place to leave shoes in the area.

Geta: Japanese footwear featuring an elevated platform and a thong.

Gozaimasu: Technically a verb, it is used after "Thank you" or "Good Morning" to make the greeting formal.

Gyokuro: A tea, one of the most expensive types of Sencha. Grown in the shade instead of sunlight.

Hai: Yes.

Hajimemashite: "Nice to meet you."

Hayaku: "Hurry up."

Matcha: A powdered green tea.

Miso: Bean paste.

Miso shiru: Soup flavored with bean paste.

Obi: Traditional sash used with kimono

Ocha: Green tea. The "O" is an honorific –
emphasizing the importance of tea to the Japanese.

Ohayo: Good morning.

Onigiri: Rice balls. These are sold everywhere, and
there are many flavors.

Ryokan: Traditional Japanese inn or guest house

.-san: An honorific title used after a name.

-sama: Also an honorific used after a name, more
formal than "san".

Sencha: A specific type of green tea. The brew is paler
than matcha.

Shinkansen: The Japanese high-speed train. "Bullet
train."

Shogun: Military ruler in feudal Japan.

Sobacha: Tea made from roasted buckwheat.

Sumimasen: "Excuse me."

Un: An informal syllable indicating agreement.

Torii: Gate at the entrance of a shrine

Watashi wa: I am. (More literally, "as for myself.")
Used to begin many sentences.

TEMPLES AND SHRINES MENTIONED

Byodoin

Heian

Hirano

Jobon Rendai-ji

Kinkaku-ji

Kyoto Gyoen Garden

Myokaku-ji

Nijojo

Ryoan-ji

Rokusonno

Shinzenko-ji

Shokoku-ji

Suika Tenmangu

Yakusana

ACKNOWLEDGMENTS

Cherry Blossom Temple is the result of a long journey. The first step? Learning about a scholarship sponsored by the national Sisters in Crime organization. For a romance writing class, of all things. As a mystery writer, I wondered about signing up for the class. "Well," I thought. "To a certain extent, writing is writing. I'm bound to learn something." I had a frank discussion with the instructor, Leigh Michaels. I told her I didn't believe I could write a traditional romance, and I described what I had in mind. She gave me the green light. Thank you, Leigh.

I also want to thank the members of Indiana Writers Workshop, who read the novel in its entirety and offered meaningful critique every step of the way. Thank you, Teri, Tony, Mark, Jeff, Steve H., Steve W., Pete, Sylvia, June, and John.

A special thanks to my husband, John, who read each chapter with an eye for detail and reaffirmed my belief in the characters I created. I want to express my gratitude to my good friend Linda, who read the book in installments and kept asking for more.

To my children and their spouses, I also am indebted. My daughter Eve and son-in-law Ariel offered professional insights that were incorporated. And to my son Ben and daughter-in-law Aoi, who provided a multitude of valuable tips concerning the cultural aspects of the story.

A special thanks to Hank Phillippi Ryan, who provided feedback on the first chapter. The stunning cover was created by Frauke Spanuth.

There are many others who influenced Cherry Blossom Temple. Writing a story of this type took me out of my comfort zone, but I made many unexpected discoveries during the process. I hope you enjoyed it.

ABOUT THE AUTHOR

C.L. Shore began reading mysteries in the second grade and has been a fan of the genre ever since. *Maiden Murders*, (2018), a prequel to *A Murder in May* (2017), is her most recent mystery release. Her short stories have appeared in Sisters in Crime anthologies, *Kings River Life Magazine*, and *Mysterical-E. Cherry Blossom Temple* is her first women's fiction novel.

Shore has been a member of Sisters in Crime for over a decade, serving as a board member for several years. A nurse practitioner and researcher, she has published numerous articles on family coping with epilepsy as Cheryl P. Shore. Shore enjoys travel and entertains a fantasy of living in Ireland for a year.